Poppies And Black Pears

Cover design by xxxxx

Book design by xxxxx

Published by Warren Nunney

Printed by Book Printing UK www.bookprintinguk.com
Remus House, Coltsfoot Drive, Peterborough, PE2 9BF

Printed in Great Britain

ISBN xxx-x-xxxxxx-xx-

Chapter 1

The cold morning air filled the room, the early morning sun creeping through the un-shuttered windows, waking him from a fitful sleep. As was always the case the last few months, lucidity was upon him almost immediately, as he surveyed the surroundings. Aware of shallow breathing behind him, Jim delicately stretched a leg out of the bed, so as not to awake the slumbering figure he had been with since late the previous evening. Fresh, morning air enveloped his legs as he stood, naked, stretching and moving across the room towards the opening that used to be a window, away from the bed. In this part of France, even this far behind the line, glass was something houses had not possessed for many months.

Looking out onto the small square, life was beginning to stir again in the small village, the last few residents clinging on to their previous life. Mixing with the British soldiers and taking advantage, in varying ways, of the relative peace and normality of the small French town at the height of war. A stirring in the bed made him turn.

'Sorry, did I wake you?'

A slow smile spread across Beatrice lips. She gently rubbed her eyes, betraying the answer she gave.

'No, not at all, don't worry'.

Eyebrows were raised, and the hint was taken as Jim turned to allow her to dress, while he feigned interest in the courtyard below the window. Soldiers washing by the water pump, locals going about their business, some interacting, some trying to pretend the army was not there at all, and life was going on as normal. Which you could convince yourself, until you took a closer look, and saw the houses were roofless, craters in the road, abandoned vehicles…. he squinted, and the blurred vision allowed him to see the town as it likely was years ago, before war, before the army. Beneath the surface, it was still there.. but would it be the same again? Like myself, he thought. Changed, worn, tired.

'I did not know the town held that much interest for you, Jim?'

He turned to see Bea in her drivers uniform, just pinning her hair.

'Sorry, miles away, you know how it is'.

'I do, and I also know I need to be back at the field hospital in an hour, so we should get a move on'.

The smile mellowed the harshness of the words, and he gave a half smile back as he crossed the room and started dragging his uniform on. He could already feel the room starting to warm up slightly, the early spring day was maybe going to supply some warmth, in comparison to the bleak winter that seemed never ending. Typical for a march back to the front line after a short diversion out of the firing line. Unease slowly crept over him, after a few hours of respite the return loomed large on the horizon.

'Bea, come on, don't pretend you're not with him!'

Giggles followed the shout from the road outside.

'I'm on my way down', she replied. Jim felt a soft kiss on his temple.

'Write. Please'.

'Of course'.

He turned and kissed her goodbye.

'You know I will miss you' .

A thoughtful look crossed her face … 'of course you will...' and then turned and left.

He heard her speak to her friend below, muffled voices, more laughter and he heard them move away. Jim gathered his few belongings together, and followed mere moments later, quickly stepping into the street, then turning and heading towards the camp and quarters.

The walk took him through the town centre, past the few cafés and restaurants he had spent some time in during the last couple of days, and back towards the camp. The walk was brief, and gave Jim time to think about the evening before, and what lay ahead.

The town got busier as he worked his way back, until the buildings gave way and fields opened out ahead of him. Fields full of tents, temporary but they seemed to have been here forever, or would be. The town was a stepping stone between home and the front line. New arrivals started here, their first real stop in France after the crossing. Veterans, of days, months or years, knew this as a staging post… stopping in reserve for a couple of days, or head back to England. On leave or injured. Or worse.

He found the tent that had been home for just a few days, Archie packing stuff away, ready for the journey back to the front line. Jim braced himself for the ribaldry after last night, but the expected abuse did not come.

'Surprised you came back, thought you would have stayed away for as long as possible?'

'You know me, always keen to get back to the fun'.

Archie looked and smiled, picking his kit up with a grunt, then walked past his returning friend.

'You've got about 5 minutes, mate. Town square'.

A few hours later and they were still on the road. Lines of soldiers slowly moved along the dirt track. The monotony evident from the way they carried themselves, shoulders down, quiet. The songs, jokes and murmur of conversation that accompanied them at the start was now fitful, if heard at all. Mile after mile of countryside, pock-marked by the signs of years of war, but not shared equally across the countryside.

As Jim moved on, he would go through a village barely touched by the conflict, houses still intact, fields around starting to fill with the crops the villagers and those around would need for the months to come. You would see the odd face, maybe children playing, a farmer in a field. Then further on, another village ravaged by the seemingly never ending barrage of men and vehicles, taking it in turns for control over what was now a skeletal village.

Looking up again from his feet and the monotonous journey, he took in what was around him for the first time in what seemed like hours. They were moving through a seemingly un-touched area of Northern France. Squinting in the morning light that had tired his eyes after hours of staring at the road, the area around him almost seemed comforting. Frowning at the discovery, he looked in more detail at the scenery, and slowly realized how reminiscent it was of his childhood home. A cluster of houses in a small valley, surrounded by fields created by god purely to be farmed, and on the top of the smallest hill, the church, over-looking its parishioners.

Chapter 2

Jim was intrigued. Left alone at home on a Sunday morning, with a list of chores to be done, while his parents joined a straggling line of thirty or so villagers walking down the single track lane. Past the village pub, and left up the hill towards the church. It was not, he realised, a particular desire to go there. He knew where they went, it was the fact he could not. Innate curiosity of a child. Or just the fact that a boy of six was not going to accept the boredom of being home on his own for very long, even with a list of chores. Walking into the small fenced garden, displaying a frown across his face, he started to pick the vegetables from the patch in the garden his father sometimes worked.

Washing them as he was shown, scrubbing the mud off, he left them in the basket in the kitchen. He was going to find out what he was missing out on. It must be fun, if the whole village went every week! Why could he not go? He had not misbehaved… he never would with the temper his father was so quick to sometimes show…he had worked that one out at an early age. Latching the back door, not that there was anything to steal in the house, or anyone around who would in this small community, he wandered up the path. Keeping low behind the bush in case anyone was still in next door, Jim rushed through the gate and down the lane. Knowing deep down he was made invisible simply by the speed at which he ran.

This was one thing he knew he could do, even at a young age, was run. Aware already of the limits of the small village of Brockton, not that much bigger than a large hamlet, and miles from the nearest town, he felt so alive when he was sprinting round the village. Everything was done at a run… down to the football field, or before he got that far left up the lane to his grandparents to help with chores, never walking. This time, he went past both usual options, and sped up the incline towards the church, and its few surrounding houses at the top of the hill. The larger houses, 'posher' he heard his mum say.

Cresting the hill, he ran right down church lane, only now slowing to a jog, sweat just starting to make an appearance on his brow. His heart beat slowly returning to normal. Only now did the first vestiges of concern and lack of belief enter his thoughts, for the first time since the acorn of an idea first appeared. What was he to do now he got here? Slowly continuing down by the hedgerow, and the larger homes, the church came into view, and as it did, the soft sound of singing.

Crouching down again, as if at that point he felt some unseen eyes on him, he crossed the road and moved towards the Norman church from which the sound was emanating. What now? He knew where they were, he could go home and it would be his secret, no one would know, something for him alone to have for himself. But that meant nothing, he wanted to see what he was missing out on. He had come this far, what was the point if he just went back again. Decision made, if ever there was a doubt, his feet slowly started moving forward again towards the huge oak doors.

He noticed the sound of the villagers singing was still going, knowing that if he was going to go in, now would be the time. Hand rising towards the iron ring handle, Jim put his weight onto it and the latch slowly rose, just enough for him to pull it forward, far enough to squeeze through and into the cool interior. Quietly closing the huge door behind him, he noticed he was at the back of the church, and the rows of pews leading off to the left. In front of him was a huge bath like item, made of stone. With everyone looking left, if he could get there and hide behind it before the singing finished, he could see everything while not being seen himself… at least that was the idea. Gently moving forward, he crawled towards the font, not noticing the hymn had come to an end, and all was silent in the church, for the first time since he had first stopped running on the road outside.

'...and the Lord God looked down...'

Jim was vaguely aware the sermon had started, and slowly peered around the font to look towards the vicar. On his left, he could see the back of his mother's head, looking intently forward, hands clasped, in her Sunday best. His mother cleaned at the larger houses at the top of the village, and his father labored on the local farms. Sunday best may have been the case a good few years ago, but not now.

His eyes moved forward, as slowly he realised the church was almost full, and most people he recognized and knew their names, at least from the back. He also noticed the clothes they wore got better as they sat towards the front. The figures in the front pew he only knew by sight, people from the top of the village, who he never saw around and about his house.

' And the devil was amongst them, and we know he makes work for idle hands....' The vicars voice was raised, and as Jim scanned the front of the church, their eyes met between the rows of pews. He froze, his heart seeming to stop, at the same time as the vicars speech paused. The scene became like a picture, as no-one moved or breathed, life taking a pause, as he could only stare at the figure in white stood before the alter and stained glass window. Then the vicar turned to face the congregation on the left, and continued with his speech. Jim took his chance and crawled back to the door, to his ears every footstep sounding as loud as a hammer blow, and fled out the church as if the devil the clergyman spoke of was on his tail.

Outside, the warmth startled him after the cool of the church. It had only been a few moments inside, but the atmosphere still seemed to lay over him. He would avoid the road going back, and cut across the churchyard and the orchard beyond, and go across the fields. The service would be over soon, and he did not wish to be seen on the road. Reverend Steed seemed to be nice, he had come to the house a few times to speak to his mother. But he also knew his grandparents hung on his every word. Jim hoped that it would be forgotten. After the event he was not even sure why he had such a desire to go, what interest was there in a church service? The longer he did not go the better, surely?

Strolling through the graveyard, acting as if it was the perfectly natural and obvious place for him to be, he checked out the names on the gravestones. Names interested him, all the families had been here for generation after generation, you heard them talk about it, boast about it. He could see names repeat, and then large family plots, for those who could afford it. His few friends in the village talked about it, houses they lived in, three or four generations, houses that had been in the family longer than anyone could remember. But there must be more outside the village, he thought. Aware, and not for the first time, that there was a whole world he heard about but was yet to see.

Snapping out of his reverie, he slowly made his way to the stile at the far end of the graveyard, the farthest point from the church. He needed to make a move on to get back in time, fear now kicking in after so long out of the house, and eased over the gate with the nimbleness typical of a young boy, living in the country. As his foot hit the ground, he heard a muffled sound coming from the plum trees to the side of the path. Or did he? He took a tentative step, but there it was again. It sounded like a sob. Someone was upset. He should see if they were alright, as his gran always said you should treat others as you wish to be treated yourself. He thought it sort of meant if you were hurt, would you want someone to help you. He decided he would, it would only take a minute, and if he ran afterwards he would still be home before the family. They would still be chatting to Reverend Steed, and then make the slow walk home. His father would doubtless insist on a drink at the pub on the way. Mum had mentioned it between gritted teeth before. Yes, Jim figured he had time. And it was the right thing to do.

He slowly moved from the path into the gaps between the trees. Just beginning to bear fruit, they would not be ready for a good few more weeks, and he would be back up then, helping to pick them. A few more steps, and another grunt, and a squeal, that stopped abruptly. Not a scream, he did not think. Unsure now, his steps faltered, but he kept moving. Someone hurt themselves, it happened. He tried to lighten his step, a light fear rising inside him.

Another step and he saw two people, stood up against the tree. He recognized them both. Bea was about nine years old, she was on the outside of his close circle of friends, but well known to Jim. One of only maybe ten or so children in the village, they all knew each other well, it being a close community. She had red marks on her face, her eyes were wide, and she was scared, Jim could see that. The other boy was pressing her against the trunk. Leaning on her. He was bigger and older, Tom, but still only twelve. He noticed Bea looking, and turned to see what had caught her attention.

'Jim, get someone, ple…' the words were cut off by the older boy slapping her face.

'Shut up!'. Looking at Jim, he spat on the ground. 'Jimmy, off you go boy, we're just playing a game'.

Bea did not look to Jim like she was happy. Indecision froze him to the spot, scared of Tom but something told him what was happening to her was wrong. He liked her, she was always nice to him, and to the other smaller kids. Jim looked up at Tom, voice wavering a little. Not sure of himself or the situation he found himself in.

'No'… coming out barely audible, but loud enough for Tom to hear.

‘You little … come here and say that’.

Tom turned to walk towards him, taking his hand momentarily off Bea, and in a blink she took her chance. Biting the other arm that still held her shoulder, Tom screamed and let go, giving her vital seconds. She ran towards Jim.

‘Run Jim, go home, quickly! Go!’

The urgency in her voice snapped him out of his lethargy, and he turned and ran, towards home, away from the scene he did not quite understand and away from the church. Unseen behind him, Bea was back on the path, but she turned towards the stile and the church! Barely seconds behind her, Tom appeared at the stile just as she landed the other side. At that point, he stopped in his tracks. Coming across the churchyard were the first of the parishioners, slowly walking through the graveyard toward the orchard.

Bea immediately saw sanctuary, and slowly walked towards them, brushing her hair and face into respectability as she walked. Tom turned to look toward the lower village, scowl covering his face, and saw Jim running, already far into the distance. Spitting into the turf, he wiped his mouth and walked back into the orchard.

Jim arrived home, having not stopped running. Soon he was in the kitchen, washing his face with cold water. His mind raced as he went over what he had seen. Knowing it was wrong, he knew he had helped Bea, and was right to help her, but he was also worried. He figured Tom would not be happy, and that there would be some sort of payback in the future.

Later that evening, as activity in the house was winding down, and Jim was wondering if he could make up a good enough excuse to stay up longer, there was a knock at the door. His eye’s looked that way, wide as saucers. His mother glanced a look at his father, un-used to visitors at this time on a Sunday, but he was asleep, in his usual Sunday state of fatigue from the week mixed with beer at the pub. Scorn embedded across her features, she got up moved to the front door, which opened direct into the living room.

'Hello, Reverend Steed, what brings you at this late hour?'

'Ah, Mrs Turner, do not worry yourself, it is just a social visit, and a short one. Would Jim still be up, or has he gone to bed?'

'No, he is here, one moment'. Turning around to call him, he had already appeared by her side upon hearing the vicars voice. 'Oh, here you are, the Reverend would like a word. Would you like to come in to talk, I may have some tea I could get you?'.

'Oh no, please don't go to any trouble' he replied, knowing full well she had enough on her hands feeding the family with the wastrel husband of hers, and probably did not even have any tea in the house 'Maybe Jim would be kind enough to chat outside with me, I do love these evenings, and I am sure I don't want to intrude'.

'Of course, off you go Jim', she replied, escorting him out with her hand on his shoulder, and closing the door behind them.

Jim knew it was about today in the church, but was unsure what tack the vicar would take. He was taken by surprise.

'Young Jim, I saw Beatrice Dunmore this morning after service' The older man sat on the wall that ran up the side of the house, and indicated that Jim join him.

'She seemed quite shook up, and after some, shall we say, gentle encouragement, she told me a story that reflected very well on you. You are but a young chap, but you still did the right thing'. He looked down at the young boy by his side. 'It may be some years to come before you work it all out. However, primarily I am here to suggest you stay away from Master Tom for the foreseeable. A lad who is most definitely making the worst of his life'. This was accompanied by a sigh. 'Steer clear, young Jim. And here is a little something for your actions today'.

From his cloak, he produced an apple, and put it into Jim's hand. Patting his head, they moved back to the door. His mother opened it, obviously not having moved far from it in the first place, held there by her curiosity.

'There you are, Mrs Turner, back safe and sound. I shall leave you and not take up any more of your time. I just asked Jim a favour, and gave him this apple as a sign of my appreciation. As of next week, Jim will come to Sunday school. He takes such an avid interest in the church, it would be wrong of me not to support that interest. He has also offered to clean the font before Sunday school next week.' With a wink at Jim, he went on. 'I noticed during today's sermon there was so much dust covering it, I could have sworn I saw a child's face forming in the stonework!' And with that, he turned and left.

Jim quickly turned and went up to his room before his mother could interrogate him, wondering on his way up the creaking, wooden stairs how much his decision to sneak into the church today would come back to haunt him.

Chapter 3

The village had a fayre every year, celebrating May Day. The whole local area got involved, including all of the surrounding cottages, hamlets and farms. With the nearest small town a good few miles away, it regularly drew a large crowd of people. The field that covered the distance between the village and up the hill towards the church was provided by the farmer for the day. Alongside the field ran the road up the hill, with the orchard on the other side towards the top. All the community provided something, there were stalls selling clothes, games for the children, and another farmer had provided a pig that was slowly roasting on a spit in the corner of the field. The local pub had taken a couple of kegs of beer outside and had set up alongside the roasting pig.

Jim was walking round with his family, his grandparents were also around somewhere, and the field appeared to be full of people as far as his eye could see. He was enjoying himself, but at the back of his mind were the two big events of the day. The village football match would be later, the annual event being more of a chance to get even for some perceived slur during the prior year, than any great show of skill or expertise.

However, before that, the maypole dance was starting to cast it's light in his mind. Jim had been volunteered, as part of Sunday school he had been caressed into joining by the vicar, to take part. At the end of each Sunday school lesson, he and the other seven children had practiced for the last few weeks, the verger playing the piano as the vicar took them through their paces, in, out, and around to the time of the music, until the ribbons got tighter and tighter until they finally formed a colourful plait down the maypole. Lots of mistakes had happened in the first few weeks, but by the end they had done it perfectly four or five times. Jim only hoped that it would be the case again, he did not want to mess up in front of the whole village at the May Day Fayre.

'Off you go' said his Mum, when some of his friends appeared, 'go and have fun, but don't forge to listen out for when you are needed for the dance'

Already she had turned to talk to one of the neighbours before the sentence had been completed, knowing the good common sense her son had even at his young age. He had heard comments before he wandered off … 'Does too much thinking that one, too quiet for my liking' … a typical example of some opinions he had heard before from people in the village. Adults seemed to sometimes think children were deaf, talking about them as if they were not there. It was a statement he had heard before many time, in various forms. Turning around, he ran over to the group of boys, all around his own age, and after much laughter and pushing, they all happily ran off round the fayre to see what mischief they could get into, before they were called to account later.

Without requiring the need to discuss the options open to them, the boys all made their way as one to the coconut shy. Bea was just walking away, and gave Jim a brief smile as their paths crossed. The memory of the orchard was growing dim in his mind after a few months, but each time he saw Bea it floated to the surface for a few moments, before disappearing back into the depths of his memory.

'C'mon Jim, your turn'. Jim turned back to see Peter offering him the wooden ball to take his turn, and within moments Bea and the orchard were forgotten. After the boys spent some time there, and finally came to the decision the coconut targets were definitely tied on to the stands, they carried on walking around the fayre, enjoying the simple fact it was a different day to any other in the year.

After what seemed like moments in his head, Jim could see the vicar on the stand to the far end of the field, announcing the start of the maypole dance. Could all the children meet at the pole as soon as they could? Just to the side, he could see his mother anxiously looking over the heads of the villagers to see if she could spot him in the crowd of villagers

Quickly he ran to the area roped off for the dance, heart racing, and took his red sash from the vicar, placing it over his shoulder and then tying it round his waist. All the other children were ready in moments, and a crowd was starting to congregate around the rope. All the group of youngsters picked up their ribbons, and took the starting position. Jim looked around, and felt his stomach start to twist and turn, the nerves finally starting to betray him as the eyes of the crowds looked on at the small group of children circling the maypole.

The verger was on the stand and started playing the accordion. The children moved off as one, dancing in and out of each other, feet not always moving exactly in time with each other, or the music, but it was close enough. As Jim moved to the outside, he saw a face staring at him from the ring of people. It passed in a blur, and he continued moving around, the ring getting tighter as the ribbons shortened with each circle of the maypole. The next time, he snatched a look again, and saw Tom in the same place. He was just staring at Jim, not moving. The music stopped, and the crowd applauded, but not Tom. He just stared, a blank look seeming to cover his face.

The children finished along with the music, and then moved off to find their parents, and hopefully receive some congratulations, as the crowds applauded before finally starting to disperse. Jim went to find his Mum forgetting to take his sash off in his hurry.

'Hello, well done! No mistakes there, I am very impressed. Did you enjoy that?'

'Yes, it was fun, I guess. Can we watch the football!' Mrs Turner raised her eyebrows.

'OK, you make your way over with your grandparents, I will see if I can drag your father away from the beer tent', she muttered, and with that she walked away.

'C'mon then, young Jim' said his granddad, putting his hand on Jims shoulder, knowing the boy would not be seen dead holding an adult's hand in front of his friends, and they walked out of the fayre towards the football pitch in the middle of the field.

Each year two teams were raised, one by the Church and one by the pub. Jim loved the football, and at least a couple of the players were very good, playing for the local town. He was told his grandfather had been good in his younger days, but Jim could not see it in the old man now… he could not imagine anyone older being younger! They reached the pitch and chose a good place to see from the halfway line, Peter coming to stand by him as his family was also close by. Around half of the people at the fayre were making their way over, and Jim could see his father and mother with them, his Dad staggering slightly. His Mum held her head up, and was looking away, but Jim could see her lips moving as she talked, and the look of embarrassment mixed with annoyance on her face. Jim looked away, feeling he had encroached on something he felt was personal for his Mum.

'Oh, bugger' his granddad grunted, 'I forgot my glasses, I can't see bugger all without them'. Looking down at his Grandson, he said 'Do me a big favour young Jim, run back to our place and grab them for me? They'll be on the kitchen table, the back doors un-latched. I know you run like the wind, young whipper-snapper, if you go through the footpath through the trees, you will be back in two shakes of a lambs tail' .

Jim faltered for a second. He liked his granddad, but the game was about to start. He looked over the pitch to the changing tent, and could see no movement. Picking up on this, his granddad did not hesitate in playing his trump card, looking sideways at his grandson. 'Look, they won't be starting for another 5 minutes, if you are back by then I will get you a bag of sweets from the stall!'

Jim looked up, deal done in his head way before the words came out of his mouth. 'Alright Granddad, I won't be long', and turned to speed away from the group around the pitch. 'Back in 5 minutes, Peter' was thrown back over his shoulder at the retreating figure of his friend, as Jim ran towards the trees and the footpath a hundred yards or so away, that led to the back of his grandparents row of houses at the top end of the village.

He had run this way many times. He spent each journey seeing how quickly he could do it, errands being run for his mum, or for his grandparents, or just using it as a short cut to see his school friends. He loved being out. Leaving the field and the fayre behind him, he entered the cool of the trees, and slowed down to a jog, making sure he did not trip on the roots and undergrowth. The path trodden down by thousands of footprints over time led through the foliage for about fifty yards, and then came out of the trees at the back of the group of houses. All around was quiet as Jim jogged along the row of buildings, finally going left at the last house, his grandparents, and jumping over the small fence. He quickly went down the garden path, past the vegetable plot his granddad doted over, across the tiny patch of lawn and on to the back door. It was quickly unlatched, and Jim strode into the kitchen, his eyes quickly becoming accustomed to the slightly darker interior after the bright sunlight outside.

Looking across the room, he saw the small table for two, that his grandparents sat at alongside the sink, and in the middle his granddad's spectacles. Springing over the tiny kitchen in a couple of steps, he snatched up the glasses and turned and fled out of the house, desperate to be back for the game. He slammed the back door shut to latch it, and immediately was sprinting back up the garden path and over the fence, then stretching his legs as he ran alongside the houses and back towards the trees.

The light and steadily increasing warmth of the day quickly gave way to the cool amidst the darkness of the trees. Moving swiftly forward, barely had his senses time to recognize the change in temperature, than he felt something hit his shin and he instantly tumbled forward, face dragging along the ground. Luckily his hand had time to automatically lift in front of him, and the palms took the brunt of the force as his body hit the floor and came to a stop. For a brief second, he did not know what had happened or where he was, dazed by the abruptness of the fall. Only seconds ago he was in his grandparents' house, now he was on the floor of the small wood, a muzzy-ness in his head, aches in his legs and arms. Jim felt dazed. He tried to get up, only to be pushed down again, face down, by a hand in the middle of his back, and he grunted as his face hit the floor again. Now he was scared, as he heard heavy breathing and a voice behind him.

'Oh dear, did little Jimmy trip? You need to be careful, running through these woods on your own' It was Tom, his voice deep and sinister, he recognized him straight way. Then the voice came closer, right alongside his ear. 'Anything would happen' The next Jim knew a booted foot had stamped on his arm, the noise of the crack as it broke accompanied by the searing pain he felt from his arm that seemed to instantly spread through his body.

He screamed in both pain and shock, and the world seemed to start to spin around as lucidity left him and his mind sought the comfort of passing out. But something inside him would not let that happen, he was alone, something deep inside told him to stay awake. Tears running down his cheeks, mingling with mud from the footpath floor, and he gritted his teeth. The air around him was now silent, Tom obviously having not delayed at the scene of the crime.

He would stay awake. His parents were in the next field. He had to get help. He looked at his arm, the area between wrist and elbow almost showing a sort of dent, and sickness flowed through him. Jim shut his eyes, no tears left, just sweat and pain… and shame? He started to control his breathing, as his granddad had taught him once before. Just last year, he had fallen out of the huge tree at the end of their garden, a boring Sunday afternoon turning into a self-inflicted challenge to see how high he could climb. It had not lasted long, the brief fall ending with Jim cutting his knee open. That had hurt. This was torture in comparison. He closed his eyes. Fear started to rise again as he heard footsteps coming closer.

'Jim! Are you OK?' He looked up and saw Bea, just a few yards away now, but running towards him. 'I saw Tom come running out of here a few minutes after you went in, and figured something had gone on'.

She had knelt down by him and had gently brushed the air out of his face, making soothing noises as she did so.

'Don't worry, I am here now. Do you think you can roll over onto your back?' Jim nodded, and slowly turned, while Bea gently cradled his broken arm. 'OK, well done. I will get this in a sling, make you comfortable, and then go and get your folks, is that OK?'.

'Yes. It hurts Bea!' Tears started to flow again, as hard as he tried to be brave in front of a girl.

'I know, it won't take long, I promise'. Un-tying the sash from around him that he had worn for the maypole dance, Bea tied it round his neck, then wrapped it loosely round his arm. 'OK, let's sit you up, this tree here, it's really close'. Jim sat up, putting all his weight on his left hand, and managed to flop against the tree.

'Thank you' he hissed through pursed lips, a sickly feeling again rising in his body.

'You're welcome, and I owe you after the orchard.' She smiled, and gave him a kiss on the forehead. 'I will go and get your Mum, I won't be long, promise'. And with that she had gone down the footpath towards the field, quickly disappearing from view into the field beyond.

Jim sat in the cool of the wood, his back resting against the trunk of the tree. He found that if he just kept his arm still, he was greeted with just a dull ache rather than the sickening pain of earlier. He started to relax and the sweat on his brow soon dried. Jim's mind wandered as he thought about the events of the last, what, 10 minutes? The fact that Tom was not nice was well known, and what he has done to Jim was obviously about the events in the orchard. Bea being there was lucky for him, especially so soon. Looking up, as his Mum appeared at the far end of the footpath, closely followed by his granddad (not his dad, he noticed), his thought were of Bea, and the warmth of the final kiss on his head she gave to him before she ran off.

Chapter 4

The arm was nicely healed within a couple of months. There being no doctor in the village, the local vet, Mr George, had a look, and announced the break a clean one, before putting the arm in a cast.

'Don't worry, Jim, you will soon be using that one again… just be careful when and where you go running next time!'

He ruffled his hair when finished and got up to leave. Jim knew his mum could not afford to pay anything to the vet, but knew over the next few months, a little would be put aside for the vet, as and when it became available. Jim himself would probably help him out for a few days in the summer, slowly paying back what the family could not afford in one way or another. He looked at the light cast on his arm, and thought about the vets comment about his running. Bea had decided while running to get his parents that it was best this was kept to themselves, so as not to cause more grief with Tom, for either of them. Jim could not decide if this was the right or wrong thing to do, and just wanted to forget the whole thing, so was happy to go along with whatever she said. He was more than happy for Bea to make the decision.

Arm healed, apart from the odd ache from time to time to remind him of what happened, life carried on as normal around the village. His time was taken up with Sunday school, then normal school during the week, when chores allowed him, and then helping with the fruit picking. Life soon filled up. He also spent a morning going on the rounds with Mr George, who served the many farms, cottages and small holdings in the area, and the range of animals on them. At the end of which, Mr George took him to one side.

'Thank you, Jim, you have been a right help! But tell your mum, there's no more need, the bills been more than paid'. Jim shook the hand that was outstretched, and ran for the farm they were on, across the field towards home. He had started off being careful on his runs, but was now back to his old self, sprinting down the field, the arm and the problems with Tom forgotten.

He burst through the back door, slamming it behind him. 'Muuuuum!' he shouted, running in to the garden. She was not there, so he turned and went into the kitchen. Also empty. The same when he moved into the front room. His Mum was sat with her head down, his Gran stood by her with her hand on her shoulder.

He paused at the door, and made a gesture to return whence he had came, but his mum had already heard him, and had looked up and turned around. Jim had never seen the look on her face before, or seen his mum so… not in control. She was the keystone in the family… his mum was the intelligent one, the worker, the person they would confide in. It was she who always found a few coins when needed, always surprised with a treat occasionally, was there when he had nightmares, or was ill. She was there when he had no friends to play with, or he was just down. Always there and always Mum. Now he looked at her, and saw sadness and a deep melancholy. But her eyes also looked bright, and her skin glowed, like a weight had been lifted. Jim knew deep down before he was told what had happened.

'Now Jim, don't get upset. We are going to be fine, we always will. But, your dad, he has gone. He will always love you…' Jim doubted this… '…but he was not happy, and has gone away'. She got up out of her chair, his grandmother watching her every step and not taking her eyes off her. She came over to Jim and cradled him in her arms, showing him the love she always had for him, but getting in return support from the son who she knew would always do the right thing, the unconditional love of a child. Jim put his arms around his mother's waist and held her, unaware of the tears starting to slowly roll down his cheeks. Tears he knew were most definitely for his mother, rather than for a father who had never really been there. They stayed like that for a few minutes, frozen together, until Jim's grandmother came over.

'Come on then, me and your Mum have got some talking to do. Your granddad will want to go for his afternoon walk in a bit, go and see him and we will catch up later'. Jim let go of his Mum, and turned round to leave the house. Then he remembered his message.

'Oh, Mum, Mr George said the bills been paid'.

'Thank you Jim, that's a weight off my mind'. His mother came over, kissed him on the forehead, and said 'Off you go, go see your Granddad, make sure you are back for tea'.

Jim wavered. It did not seem right leaving his Mum when she was so upset, but his gran soon shooed him away.

Leaving the house behind, along with the conversations he would doubtless struggle to completely understand, he walked up the village to his grandparent's house. He did not feel like running. He was not sure how to feel. He could see his mother was upset, but equally he could see she already seemed happier. Or was he mistaken? His father was not there more than he was around, so to Jim it made very little difference whether he was home or not. It would mean less slaps or punches when his dad had been to the pub, and come back to find Jim guilty of some minor misdemeanor. But he was his dad. And he knew he worked and brought money to the family. Jim stopped. How would they cope? He could not understand everything that was going on, but a feeling of unease came over him, and he knew from that moment he knew he had changed forever. He could just not decide if it was a good thing or not yet. Maybe his grandfather could help. He looked up, and ran up the road towards the house, ran away from the scene of the change, and towards the comforting companionship of his grandparent.

The front gate slammed behind him, as Jim ran up, barely pausing as he entered through the back door.

'I recognize that slamming door, I am in the back garden, young Jim' came a shouted voice. Jim carried on through the house and into the back garden. His granddad was halfway up the path outside, walking towards the end of the garden, and stopped halfway to turn and look back. 'I wondered how long before you turned up. Fancy a walk? But none of that running, a walks more than enough for me these days'.

Jim smiled and walked up the path, knowing his granddad was still walking at least ten miles or so each day, going fruit picking, or to the signal box on the railway line to catch up with his old workmates.

'Just fancied a walk to the bridge, you OK with that?' he asked Jim, and knowing the answer would be positive, turned and led the way up the path, over the fence and onto the field behind the house.

Jim followed, and caught up with his granddad a few yards along the bridle path on the edge of the field, and started walking alongside him. A hand came up and ruffled his hair, as they moved along the edge of the field in companionable silence for a few minutes, round the corner and forward along the length towards the back lane at the other end. Jim studied the hawthorn hedge on his left, and thought to himself it would not be long before he would be back along here picking blackberries.

'Won't be long now will it Jim?' said his granddad, reading his mind.

'Nope, I can't wait!'

Fred Turner chuckled, and carried on walking. He loved his only grandson, and knew there was a fine man in there waiting to develop and grow. He was quiet, but he could see he was clever.

He picked things up quickly, thought about things, and when they were alone he was always asking… question after question. But he was quieter this afternoon, and Fred knew why. In his humble opinion, apart from this lad, nothing worthwhile had ever come out of his good for nothing father. But that did not change the situation, and how the boy would be feeling. They walked for a few minutes, now three quarters of the way across the field, and Fred decided it was as good a time as any to bring the subject up, afraid to let it fester longer than needed.

'You've seen your Mum and Nan then?'

'Yes'.

'What are you thinking? 'He looked sideways at the boy, who stared at the ground in front of his feet intently. 'You can tell me, you know it's always between us young-un'

Jim looked up at his Granddad, and tried to work out which of the questions to ask. Which meant more, or which would make him feel better knowing the answer. They had already reached the style at the other end of the field, jumped up and over it and turned left onto the track.

'Why did he go?'

The question Fred was expecting. And most likely because the child thought it was somehow his fault. Fred looked away, towards the railway bridge a mile distant, to collect his thoughts, and then back at Jim.

'Your father was not happy. With life, mind, nothing to do with you or your mother. I knew him for a few years before you were born, and he was not a bad man at all. Had friends, had a decent job on the farm. He always liked your mother, and it was no surprise they got together.' He paused, and looked around for a moment. 'Let's sit here a minute, lad, rest my old legs'. They sat on the five bar gate that led to the field on the opposite side of the road. Jim leant against his granddad.

'Then just after you were born, there was an accident on the farm. Your dad broke his arm..' .. at this Jim looked at his own arm…'and that was the start of things going wrong. Your dad could not work for a few months, so there was no money coming in, and a new baby. He did what he could while the break healed, but what little he made went on drink, to ease the pain. Then when he was back to work full time, the more he earned the more he drank.'

Fred sighed and put his hand on Jim's head again. 'Your father, believe it or not, was a very proud man. He had big ideas when you arrived, wanted to get his own smallholding, be able to support you all properly. But the drink stopped all that. I think he has moved away, I don't know where. A guess would be down south, try and start again.' Fred stood up, and Jim took his cue. 'He will be fine, I don't doubt, and will start again, try to change.' Fred held his grandson's hand gently, and lowered his voice, wanting him to listen. 'The important thing is you will be alright. Your Mum knows what she is doing, me and your Gran will help. We will all take care of each other'.

With that, he started walking on. They turned right and started up the lane towards the railway bridge and the signal box, stride increasing as they moved away. Fred was not sure if he had said too much or too little, only time would tell. Children bounced back at that age.

'Will he come back?' … the question came tumbling out of Jim unexpectedly. Fred took a moment with his thoughts, not wanting to destroy any hope in the lad, but not wanting to lie either.

'Maybe, maybe not. You never know. But my advice is to worry about you and your Mum. You are all that matters now'. Jim felt a tear make its way down his cheek. He was not sad, just unsure of what lay ahead, despite his granddad's words. How would they cope? Was it really not his fault? Fred took a sideways look at the boy, and figured there had been enough talk. Nothing would change now.

'Why don't you run to the bridge?' his granddad said 'That's what you usually do with me, from this tree. I will count, put your arm up when you get there. Ready…steady… go!' Jim was off like a shot, his legs pounding the road as he sped towards the bride. Fred counted in his head, while thinking about the conversation. Would they be alright? He hoped so. It was close knit community, there was work around, and the church would help. It would be hard, but life was hard. Jim needs to get used to it, sooner or later.

Looking ahead, an arm shot into the air, and Fred waved back, smiling. The lad was quick, he gave him that. Then he stretched his own legs and pushed himself on to quickly catch up with his grandson, who to all intents was now effectively his son, he thought suddenly. That thought alone making him feel his age even more than he usually did, Fred caught up with Jim before long. When his granddad arrived, Jim opened the steel gate to the right of the bridge. There, a path led along the field and down to the signal box on the railway line, and they set off along it.

Chapter 5

Jim slammed the door behind him and ran up the path. The walk to the school in the next village took a good thirty minutes, and he was already late. Embarrassment was etched across his face, as he had had this conversation with his mother only last night.

'Schools the most important thing! It may not seem it, but you make sure you put the effort in. You can help me afterwards, if you like'. Jim had listened with one ear at the time as he made his way to bed. A little over four years before, after his father's departure, they had moved back in with his mother's parents. They could not afford to stay in the small cottage on just his mother's small wage. The village had helped, as much as they could, but they were fighting a losing battle. Reverend Steed had helped, and neighbours had done what they could, the community pulling together as they always did. But it had hurt his mother, he could see. Their own house, the family home. Theirs.

He knew from talking to her over the years, she had taken it as some sort of failure, that it was all her fault in some way. But regularly over the following weeks, he had heard the same conversation between his grandmother and mother at night, when they thought he was in the bedroom he now shared with his mother, at her parent's house.

'He left you, not the other way. If it wasn't for the drinking and the lying, things may have worked out. But they didn't. It's happened, you can't change the past, love. You are here as long as you want or need to be, and that lad will be looked after'. Always words along the same lines, his grandmother knitting and his mum sat listening.

Jim still felt maybe it was down to him… some guilt gnawing away deep down. He guessed it would always be there, and just moved on, or tried to. Working at weekends for the vet, Mr George, for a couple of shillings, and doing odd jobs where and where he could, they were coping. As people did.

At the corner, he could see Peter waiting for him, looking as scruffy as always! A couple of the other children, a few years older, were a hundred yards or so further along the road already.

'C'mon Jim, can't be late again', Peter turned to start walking as soon as he greeted his friend, and they began to move along the road, walking in the opposite direction to the church. Jim had known Peter for as long as he could remember, but over the last few years, what had initially just been a group of children from the same village had developed into some closer relationships, and the bond between Peter and Jim was particularly strong. The same age, they complimented each other in a lot of ways, but disagreed on enough subjects to keep the friendship interesting. Peter Taylor's father worked in the signal box on the local railway line, and the friendship with Jim's granddad had led to the boys spending more time together as they grew up in the village.

The early morning April sun warmed the boys as they headed off along the road to the next village. Thick woodland on the right made a stark contrast to the fields on the other side of the road, full of wheat and barley reading for harvesting in the coming weeks. Hopefully I might get some work in the afternoons, he thought as he let his gaze wander over the countryside around him. The peace of the morning was only broken now and then by the occasional horse and cart, moving to or from the market town eight miles distant, passing the boys as they stretched their legs, slowly eating up the ground between them and the school.

'Whad'ya think, Jim? We gonna be alright ? My brother says the new master here is vicious. Only have to look at him and it's the cane'. Jim could hear the concern in his friend's voice, but knew things would likely not be that bad. It rarely was.

‘No, its all story, likely he will just set the standard early with the trouble makers, keeps the rest of us in line. We will be fine, couple of months and we will be done’. He punched his friend on the shoulder, and looked ahead. ‘Come on’, he suggested, ‘let’s run for a bit and catch up with the others’.

If nothing else, he knew it would take Peter’s mind off the coming morning. Without waiting for an answer, he gently broke into a jog, and soon heard his friend’s footsteps following quickly. They jogged alongside each other a short way, and caught up with the group ahead just by the Manor House, the half-way point between the villages. He had not mentioned it since they met on the corner, but Jim had recognized Bea in the group ahead. Just as they were a few yards away, Jim slowed down to a stop, just as the older girl at the back of the group turned around.

‘Ah, Mr Turner, nice to see you. It could be that you arrive on time today?’ Bea looked at him with a frown furrowing across her brow, but Jim could see a playful smile emerging as she spoke. He could feel himself flushing, and spoke to cover his embarrassment.

‘Sorry, Miss Dunmore, it won’t happen again’. A gentle laugh eased out of her mouth.

‘I am sure it won’t’.

Jim heard a mutter from Peter just behind him, but chose to ignore it. He ran so he could chat to his friend, so was not going to waste one of the few opportunities he got.

‘How is it going now, Miss? At the school, I mean?’ Bea had been working at the small village school helping the teachers there since she left school. She was hoping to continue her education if she could, but to do that she needed money. To that end, she helped at the school in the mornings, and in the afternoons she took care of the younger children at the Manor House. Jim knew the village was not enough for Bea, she wanted to move away, wanted to see the world. He liked Bea, and he really hoped she got her wish. Just not yet.

'Well,'.. She replied, in a conspiratorial voice…'the new master is not as bad as he seems. Just keep your head down and don't get involved with the class clowns'. She looked at him. 'You don't have long left, learn what you can, try and make the most of it'. With that, she smiled again and moved forward to the front of the group, with the school appearing a few hundred yards in the distance.

'Am I allowed back now, or are you still in a daze' said Peter behind him. Jim slowed down as his friend caught up and walked alongside.

'She's nice, that's all'.

'Well, I supposed if you accidentally break your arm again, at least she is still around' suggested Peter, repaying the punch on the arm received earlier. Jim smiled, and they walked the shortening distance to the school.

That evening, Jim sat in his grandparents' kitchen, while the evening meal was served. He still thought of it as being their kitchen, despite the years they had been there since his father left. This in part came from his mother, who still longed for a place for Jim and herself to call their own. She knew in her heart it was unlikely to happen anymore, strong as the desire was. She was older now, thirty two come the winter, and she knew the chances of being able to afford their one place on their own were too small to even be considered. She would likely stay in this house when her parents died, paying the small rent to the railway company that her father worked for all his life.

'Can I help you, Mum?', she offered again, as she did almost every night since they had first moved back in, knowing the answer that would come back, but still feeling she was a lodger in the house after all this time.

'All done here, don't you worry. Can you take the plates over, love, thank you' came the reply.

She got up, took the plates from the cupboard, and laid them in their place, on a table barely large enough for four that had seen better days. As she finished, and went back to her place, Fred came into the room, newspaper under his arm.

'About time, I called you a while ago' muttered his wife Mabel, 'I'm not here to wait on you, Fred Turner!' she scolded. Fred winked at Jim.

'My apologies, dearest'. Mabel brought the pans over one by one and served the meat and veg onto the plates.

'Eat it before it gets cold'.

'Sit down, Mum'.

'I'm coming, don't you worry'. She sat down and a soft silence fell on the room. Fred looked at Jim out of the corner of his eye.

'How was school lad? Still learning or have you had enough yet?'

'It was good, the new master's a bit strict, but his bark's worse than his bite I think', Jim replied, barely pausing in his eating. Fred was not so easily put off.

'And how's his assistant? She strict at all? Or is she really nice to some and not others?'

'Fred Turner, you leave the lad alone!' butted in Mabel, while Jim started to flush.

'Just asking, my dear!' Fred's voice was full of fake remorse, to un-trained ears. Jim focused on his food, the hunger of a twelve year old who could never get enough. Fred took another tack, the role of an aging cupid.

‘Do me a favour tomorrow, Jim lad. The cook at the manor house has asked for some veg to be delivered, early evening tomorrow. I was going to meet some of the lads in the pub for a chat’. Fred ignored Mabel looking up from her plate, eyes thunderous.

‘If you could pop it round there, would be a great help, she knows how much it is’. Fred used every inch of his garden for growing, as many vegetables as possible, and sold what could not be kept to have some extra money coming in. He had the knack for gardening, and many neighbours came round asking for carrots, cabbage or potatoes, and either paying with cash or in other ways, clothes, fruit, the odd pheasant they had ‘found’ in the woods.

‘Yes, of course I can’ said Jim.

‘Splendid, thanks lad. You never know, the young girl who takes care of the little ‘uns at the house finishes around then, you could maybe walk her home’. There was no interruption from Mabel this time, just food put in her mouth and eyes staring at the ceiling, while Fred carried on eating with a smile flickering across his lips. But Jim did not mind, it was exactly what he was planning to do anyway, now he had a good excuse. He just had to get his chores done as fast as possible when he got home.

Chapter 6

The period of nice weather had given away overnight, and the morning had been cloudy and cooler. Fred opined that there was rain in the air, as Jim got ready to go to school, while Mabel took an opposing view, purely so that she could disagree with her husband, Jim thought. As he exited through the back door, he left them to their friendly argument, which he figured was one of the things that kept them happy and together, comfortable in each other's company.

The school morning had gone by very quickly. The new master, who had been described as a mix of an army sergeant and the devil himself, was typically humane in the flesh, although he did not take fools gladly in the classroom. Jim actually found his teaching far more interesting than in previous years, but as much as he enjoyed study, he was still aware his role was to go out and get work, and now to support his mum, and he was sure at some point in the future, his grandparents. The walk home at lunchtime with Peter was done at high speed as usual, with the customary ribbing of each other, before they neared home, and the prospect of more chores silenced the joking and chatting until they parted in the middle of the village, going their separate ways.

The first half of the afternoon was spent helping the verger in the churchyard. Since his summons to Sunday school all those years previously, Jim had kept it up, finding he enjoyed spending time with Reverend Steed. Thinking about it, it was not so much that he felt particularly religious, but the old man just seemed very relaxed. He had obviously experienced a great deal in his life, Jim hearing about his time in Africa in his youth, from his grandparents and other villagers, and he seemed able to talk to anyone.

And he did not preach, which to Jim seemed a most unlikely skill for a man of the cloth to inhabit. Surely that was his job? As part of his chores and admittance to Sunday school, Jim also agreed to help tend the graveyard. It was one of those jobs that was never really finished, as there was always something to do, but he enjoyed the work, it was in the open air and it gave him time to think, and to be alone when he needed it. He looked around as he worked, enjoying the quiet and stillness, and the views that extended for miles.

He was mid thought and staring into the middle distance when the verger walked over, Jim not noticing until a soft voice broke the silence.

'That'll do Jim, I have a feeling the rain is on its way, you get home and we can carry on with this next week'. He dropped a small coin into Jim's hand.

'Thank you, sir', responded Jim, and immediately walked towards the end of the graveyard and the orchard beyond. Climbing the stile, Jim could vaguely remember the time he saw Tom and Bea, but over the years, the memory of a six year old boy became stretched and vague, with Jim still not really grasping what he had seen. Burying it deep down in the recesses of his mind, not wanting to consider it. He purposely did not look left as he followed the path through the slowly darkening orchard, and quickened his pace as he remembered again his promised favour to his granddad, not that he saw it as a favour in any shape or form.

Coming out the other side of the orchard, Jim climbed the second stile and came to the road. He heard a snap behind him, and quickly twisted his head round. Seeing nothing on the path behind him, he turned ahead again, crossing the road and walking down the other side towards the bottom of the village. He again felt someone's presence, and for the second time in a few minutes he stopped walking and looked around. This time he saw a dark figure behind him, that stopped moving as soon as he did, about thirty yards away. He turned, walking quickly, so as not to look afraid, but knowing just from the silhouette who it was. He would not run.

He would not be scared. He would walk normally to his grandparents. There is no rush.

As he got to the centre of the village, a voice said 'See Ya, Jim'… he turned and saw Tom walking in the other direction, towards the other end of the village. Not sure what had been going on, or why, Jim tried to push it from his mind, and quickly ran up the road to his grandparents' house, and straight in through the back door. He would not think about what had just happened, if indeed anything had, until he had done what he had to do. Opening the door, he realized his heart was beating fast, and a slight sweat had come on his forehead, which he knew had nothing to do with the walk or run he had just had. Closing the door behind him, Jim took a few seconds to wipe his forehead, and let his heart beat return to normal. He then slowly walked through the house into the back garden, to pick up the vegetables that had to be taken to the Manor House.

His grandparents were nowhere to be seen out in the back, but Jim could see a basket of vegetables with a note left on top of it by the fence on the left. It was full of carrots, potatoes and some turnips. As he lifted the basket, pleasantly surprised to notice that it was nowhere near as heavy as it looked, he looked towards the west and saw some thicker clouds developing. The rain looked to be getting closer. A tapping sound made him turn around, and he noticed his grandmother at the kitchen window, which she proceeded to open.

'Don't stand their gawking lad, get a move on! That rain will be here in an hour or so, I don't want your wet clothes making a mess in my house, I've already mopped the floor three times because of your Granddad!' and with that her head disappeared back into the house. Jim smiled to himself, but he took her advice and quickly went back through the house, latching the door behind him, before striding down the front path and down the street towards the road.

Turning right, he took his usual route towards the school, knowing that this time the journey should be no more than ten minutes at the most to the Manor House door. The wind slowly picked up as he moved, and he noticed the men in the fields moving around and making their way towards the road. The working day was almost done, and no one wanted to be caught in the rain that was rolling in from the horizon. As his stride lengthened, for the second time that night perspiration appeared on his brow. But this time, though, it was again not due to the physical effort he was making, but the air was more humid, and the realization a storm was brewing made Jim quicken his stride even further.

Turning off the road and down the drive towards the house, he was almost at a jog, and then slowed down as he neared the house. A large Georgian building, set in acres of its own fields, and owned by the local lord of the manor, who to Jim's knowledge spent most of his time in London and only came back during the summer. But his family remained most of the time, and Bea looked after the two young children. Stepping round the front of the house and round the back, Jim arrived at the servant's entrance, and rang the bell, just as he noticed the first spot or two of rain starting to fall. The maid answered the door, and Jim asked for the cook.

'From Fred Turner, Miss' he stated, as the cook arrived at the door.

'Ahh, that's splendid, I can always rely on Fred. Here's the money, lad, and thank Fred for me'. Jim took the money, but did not move yet, trying to work out in his mind how to see Bea… this was one thing he had not done. 'Yes, lad, is there anything else?' questioned the cook, looking at him.

'Yes, Miss Dunmore, is she in?' Another spot of rain fell on his cheek, bringing down with it a bit of inspiration. 'It's going to be a storm and is getting dark, I thought I should walk her home?'

The cook smiled 'That's a nice idea lad, she leaves about now, let me get one of the girls to see if she is ready'. She disappeared back into the house, leaving Jim on the doorstep and shutting the door. Seconds passed that seemed like minutes, and more drops of rain fell. Jim looked up at the sky, to see how long they had, and at that point the door opened. He jerked his head back and Bea was in the doorway.

'Hello Jim, nice of you to walk me, much appreciated'. She turned to shut the door, and took a look at the sky. 'I think we may get wet, let's get a move on shall we?' He offered her the crook of his arm, having seen his granddad do this in church for is gran. Bea smiled and took his arm, and they quickly walked back down the drive.

'I did not bring a coat or umbrella today, not sure why', she muttered as they quickened the pace. Jim turned to reply, but whatever he was about to say would have been drowned out by the crash of thunder, that seemed to be the starting pistol for the deluge of rain that enveloped them as they moved along out of the drive and along the road. They instinctively broke into a run without needing to discuss it first, but after a few yards they knew it was a waste of effort. The rain was running down the road and they could barely see more than twenty yards in front of their faces.

Jim knew there was a barn in the field, and was just raising his head to look for it and make the suggestion when Bea dragged him off to the left and to the five bar gate that led to it. Bea was over in a second, Jim following on her heels, and they both reached the barn on the other side at the same time. It just housed two ploughs that the shire horses dragged, so there was space for them to move along the wall to the back, out of the wet. Bea looked at him and smiled.

'Sorry to drag you like that, no time to ask!'

It was dry in the barn, although their clothes were already pretty wet from the few minutes they spent in the rain. She looked out quickly at the sky, and then looked at Jim.

'Let's give it a few minutes, I am not going out in that!' Bea ducked her head back in, and looked around. Her eyes spotting a flat surface on the back of the plough, she moved over to sit down, running her hands through her hair in what she knew was a doomed attempt to get it as dry as possible. She looked at Jim and smiled. 'I don't know why I bother, this rain does not look like stopping, we may just have to make a run for it', raising her eyebrows in resignation.

Jim smiled back, and turned to look outside, to give himself something to do, a few seconds to get composed. He had been almost mute since the moment he had collected Bea from the Manor House. He had noticed this over the years, whenever they met. Sometimes they just talked, and chatted, and he could have been with anyone, anywhere. Any semblance of shyness overcome just by the awareness of being with someone he just felt so comfortable with. At other times, he could not speak, did not know what to say, and could barely look at Bea. Unfortunately this seemed to be one of those times. Jim had felt the sickly, lurching feeling in his stomach from the moment he left his grandparent's house and started walking along the road. He looked up at the sky, as if trying to find inspiration, when Bea's voice interrupted his thoughts.

Behind him, she had watched and been aware of his reticence. She had known him all his life, and knew that the sometimes quiet, shy boy was also one of the most mature and intelligent for his age at school. Bea believed he had the ability to better himself, but like her he was hemmed in by the confines of the village. Single mum and old grandparents that she knew he would end up supporting, when he was capable of so much better.

'Do you still have any problems with Tom?'

Jim turned, snapped out of his reverie and looked at Bea. This was not a question he expected, and after this afternoons events it came as a surprise.

'Not really, I guess'. He frowned, and then moved his way over to sit alongside Bea, his confusion at how to talk brushed away in an instant. He could always talk to her. 'I was up at the graveyard today, and walked back by the orchard path, just as it was getting dark. Someone followed me, but at a distance, until we got to the village. Then he spoke, and it was Tom.' Jim shrugged in the semi darkness. 'Maybe it was nothing, no reason for him not to be out, and he never came near me'. He looked at Bea. 'But It has happened, every now and then. Like…' he shook his head, pausing to consider and think what he thought was the motive in the other boy…'he is just letting me know he is there, I guess'.

A silence developed for a minute, both thinking about what he had said. The rain continued to lash down onto the roof of the barn, and it was almost like night outside.

'You were very brave, that day in the orchard'. Jim looked at the floor, waiting for Bea to continue. 'You were so young, but you did the right thing, even in your innocence. I don't think even now you know how important it was what you did, and I will always remember it'.

Jim flushed. Over the years it had been briefly mentioned before, but this felt different, the tone of Bea's voice. He kept looking down, for fear of seeing the look in her face, and thinking it may help her if he did this.

'He has not touched me since…or come near me, really. It's like a secret between the three of us, keeping all three safe in some way. But you got hurt, and I am so sorry for that. I hate that I could not stop it happening'. She paused. 'Anyway, the good news is, for us and the village, is Tom is going'. Jim looked up, and saw Bea wiping her face. Tears, or rain, or a mixture of both. 'Yes, he is joining the army. The farmers round here have slowly tired of his laziness and drinking' . At this Jim thought of his Dad, but quickly pushed the image aside. 'And he is joining the army.' Bea's voice was now her own again.' Avoid him for a couple of months, that's all we need to do.' Jim got up, walked to Bea and hugged her. He felt awkward, and confused if he was doing the right thing. But Bea said nothing, and they just held each other, as the rain slowly started to ease.

Bea let go and got up, turning away to wipe her eyes again and dry her hair and face. Jim turned and walked to the door, looking up. The rain was starting to slow, finally, and the sky was getting brighter in the west. He looked at Bea.

'I think we can go, it's still raining, but it's a lot slower, probably will be finished by the time we get back, I think.'

'Good job, I have plenty to do at home, and now have these wet clothes to try and get dry'.

She walked towards him, and the left the barn, climbed the gate and started the short journey back to the village, content in their silence and company. As they reached the village, Bea would head left to her own family home.

'Don't forget, Jim, a few weeks more. Avoid him if you can'. She gave him a brief kiss on the cheek, and had turned to walk home without a backward glance. Jim's eyes followed her for a few seconds, then he too headed towards his grandparents, now aware for the first time since he first left home how wet he was, and focusing on getting into the warm and dry.

Chapter 7

The weeks eased by, as spring moved slowly towards summer. Jim's time was spent at school in the mornings, his last few months, and doing different jobs in the evenings. Work was still either with Mr George, the vet, or working in the fields and in the orchard. Any odd jobs that needed doing Jim was there, along with the other boys of his age, who were still in the village or surrounding hamlets.

Most of the surrounding area was agriculture, but there was only so much work that could be offered each year, and the work that was on offer dried up during the winter. It was a case of making what you could while the sun shone, and then putting by what was possible to keep you going during the winter months. If no work was around locally, the boys would move away towards the local towns or even further afield to the cities. Jim knew some older boys who had gone further afield, to Birmingham or the towns further north, looking for work in the mills and mines. For the girls it was the life of a servant for most, or staying at home raising a family.

The work that Jim enjoyed most was with the vet. He had an affinity with the animals, and enjoyed working with them, large and small. Most of the work was on the farms, and man and boy travelled fair distances at times. Jim would be sat alongside Mr George on the pony and trap, and during the journeys the older man would try to teach Jim as much as he could. He knew Bill George was grateful for this help, and was trying to pass on as much of his knowledge as he could. But he also knew that there was unlikely to be anything for him when he finished school. He needed to be able to study further, but that was not going to happen. His grandparents and mother barely made enough for them to get by, and what Jim earned was not going to pay for an education. He also knew that Mr

George himself was struggling to get by, like most people he had his own allotment to feed himself as much as he could.

From his time spent helping, Jim knew what the farmers could be like, calling in the vet at the last minute, only if they had to, as they also struggled for money. They would rather go by the old wives tales handed down over the years, for how to treat each illness in each animal. Often, by the time Mr George was called in, it would be too late, and thus the farmer had the vet to blame. Jim sighed, thinking about the times that had happened in the last few weeks. He would help the vet for as long as he could, for the few pennies he could get.

They were coming back on Saturday morning from one of the smallholdings and Jim was being dropped off by the church to see if any work needed to be done in the orchard, before going home. Climbing down from the seat by the older man, his eyes quickly surveyed the church and the surround area, looking for the verger or the reverend, and he set off towards the side of the church that led to the graveyard beyond.

'Hold your horses, youngster' said Mr George stepping down from the trap. Jim stopped mid-stride and turned back guiltily.

'Sorry sir, I was in a rush… thank you for letting me help today'.

The vet chuckled. 'Don't you worry about that, you know you're a help to me, and good company too, truth be told'. He reached into his pocket and took out a coin. 'That's for your work this week, thank you lad'. The coin was flicked in the air and Jim caught it with one hand as it spun and fell towards the floor. 'Wander over Monday, if you are free, and we will see if we can't get you busy again' the older man said with a wink. 'Oh, and how's that arm of yours, still good?'

Jim held it up as if showing off something precious. 'Does not ache at all, not for a long time. You should have been a doctor, Mr George!' he replied, with a grin.

'Cheek will get you nowhere, lad,' chuckled Mr George. 'Take care, and ask after your Mum for me when you see her'. With that, he walked the horse to the end of the lane, round and back towards the road, with a brief wave as he went past the boy.

Jim turned and ran towards the church, round the corner and into the graveyard beyond. The weather was warmer now June was upon them. The grass in the yard was lush and rich after the odd showers that had fallen recently, and everything seemed fresh and vibrant with the summer sun reaching every part of the graveyard. As he looked around, he saw the figures of the verger and Reverend off to the left, and made his way over, being careful to follow the paths between the graves, having once received the admonishment of the reverend for walking over the graves by the shortest route, in his childish enthusiasm. As he got closer, the taller man looked up at the sound of being approached.

'Good afternoon, young Jim', called Reverend Steed while Jim was still a few yards away. At this point the verger also looked and smiled, acknowledging the approaching boy. 'How was it with Mr George today? How many of our good Lord's animals did you save today…' a pause…' or not, as the case me may?', which was accompanied by a comedic, questioning look on the curate's face, with a flicker of smile.

'All good today, nothing lost' laughed Jim.

'Glad to hear it. Now, before you ask, there is nothing for you to do today, though I appreciate you coming up. The verger and I were just discussing the services for next week, then I am off to visit some of my older villagers who are in need of some support'. He walked over and rested his hand on Jim's shoulder. 'I shall see you in Sunday School tomorrow, but for today …' at this he looked down into Jim's eyes…'Go and have fun! I know Peter is in the orchard, he will likely be finished soon.' The Reverend looked askance at Jim. 'You can't do everything for everyone Jim, even I have to admit that sometimes'. The old man appeared to be lost in his own thoughts for a moment, then suddenly aware it was very quiet, he looked at Jim again. 'You're a good lad, but you need to do things for yourself, as well as others. I will see you tomorrow', and with that he turned and walked back to speak to the verger.

Jim turned and moved back towards the main path through the graveyard, thinking about what the reverend had said. It was alright to say have fun, and do things for yourself. But he was the man of the house now, he had to do these things. Who else would? It was his responsibility. Frowning thinking about it, he reached the path and veered left, towards the far end of the graveyard and the stile leading into the orchard. He had no other jobs today, it was true, maybe he would find Peter, then go home. If his Mum was ok with it, they could go and play football, or walk to the railway bridge. But only if there were no jobs to do.

Peter had been working in the orchard fruit picking that Saturday morning, with his father. Jim walked along the rows of trees, all egg plum in this first section of the site, and a couple of the villagers were still working in there, the last punnet or basket being completed before they could stop for a short lunch break. All the faces were familiar to him, and a few nods and grunts were directed his way as he went past, people focused on their work. Toward the end of the first row of trees, he saw his friend, and walked over to greet him.

Peter!'

His friend's face looked up from what he was doing. His job today, Jim knew, as he did this job himself a lot of the time he was up here, was to go up and down the lines, collecting the baskets from the workers and taking them to the owner at the far end, to be weighed and loaded onto the horse and cart. Each punnet or basket was marked against the row, and who was working in that row. The owner, Mr Taylor, a large rubicund man from spending all of his life outdoors, kept a log of who worked what part, and how much each row and tree had produced. A jolly man, to Jim's eyes, and a good boss, but like so many landowners and employers, a man to be treated with respect.

'Hello Jim', responded his friend, 'you not working in the churchyard today?'

'Nope, think most of the jobs are done, and Mr George doesn't need me'. He looked up and down the lines, as people slowly climbed down ladders, filling and picking up baskets to bring to Peter. 'You finished here? I think I will be free later?' Peter looked up and down the line, and across to Mr Taylor.

'Yes, give me half an hour, shall I call on you after lunch? I will see if I can swizz a couple of apples off old Taylor.'

'You can try!', uttered Jim, smiling 'I will see you later', and turned to go back down the row of plum trees toward the footpath.

He was thinking again walking home, about what to do. He liked his work with the vet, and fruit picking was alright while it lasted, but that was only for a few months a year. He enjoyed helping out at the church, but again, that was not a job. He needed a job, and there was nothing obvious that was calling him. Unlike a lot of the children his age, he enjoyed school, and loved reading. His Granddad had some shelves on the wall at home, a very random selection of things he had picked up over the years… so a well-thumbed Dickens would appear alongside a copy of Bradshaws Handbook. But his favourites were the Jules Verne novels they had. Not that reading novels would get him a job, he thought bitterly. His frustration seemed continuous these days.

He reached the end of the path, and climbed the gate to the road, crossing and heading down towards the village. The sun was at its height now, and Jim could feel the sweat start to trickle down his back, from the nape of his neck. Whatever he and Peter got up to, it would not be football! Far too warm for that!

Jim wiped his forehead, and heard the shuffle of feet behind him. As much as he knew who it was without looking, he had to glance behind. Turning, and there, walking down the road a good thirty paces behind him, was Tom.

'Mornin' Jim lad' was uttered from his mouth as soon as Jim's eyes settled on him. Jim turned away, but kept his pace the same. It was daylight, he was close to the village, and did not want to appear scared. The figure behind kept pace with him, no closer, no further away. Jim reached the village and turned right, heading towards the centre and then on and up towards his grandparents. As he went through the middle of the village, a voice called 'Afternoon, Jim', and the footsteps receded into the distance.

Jim kept up the same pace, and was soon at his Grandparents' house, and in through the back door. He headed straight into the back garden, too hot to stay inside, and he needed to sit and think. His granddad had an old bench at the top of the garden, made of an old railway sleeper he had 'borrowed' when working on the railway. Jim walked up the garden, and sat down with a thump, emitting a deep sigh as he did. What was Tom up to? They had barely exchanged nods when in each other's vicinity for years, now twice in no more than a couple of months he had been followed, same way, same road, but with no attempt to talk, or shout, or worse. He knew that Tom was trying to scare him, but why. Why now, when he had already taken his revenge, if that's what it was?

'Weight of the world on your shoulders, lad?

Jim looked up with a start. So fixated on what was happening, he had not even noticed his granddad knelt down in the garden, weeding round the vegetables. Weeding as a way of avoiding being given any jobs by his Gran, Jim thought.

'What's that Tom been up to now?' His granddad was looking him straight in the eye.

'How do you know its Tom?'

'Well, you came walking up the path, looking neither left nor right, sat down with a face like thunder, and spent half a minute rubbing that old broken arm of yours', Fred said pointing, and slowly getting to his feet, with a grunt. 'These knees are past it lad, think I will have to speak to Mr George and see if he can't swap mine with yours, seeing as he did such a good job with your arm.' Jim smiled, and Fred went walking over to where his grandson sat, confusion and sadness etched on his face. 'Can tell me, y'know… between us, you know that… if you don't want to go worrying our ladies in the house?' Jim nodded, and looked at his arm, and then up again at his granddad.

'How do you know Tom did this?' Jim whispered, indicating his arm by lifting it slowly. 'Bea and I kept it secret, told you I fell in the woods. Because ..' he paused, unsure how much to say without Bea's knowledge…'because Tom is a bully'. Fred took a moment, looking from his grandson to the house, where he could see Mabel in the kitchen, making bread.

'Lad, you were young, and we had our suspicions that you wanted to keep it a secret. So we let you both do that. We knew if either of you wanted to say something, you would, or if you didn't, well, it would stay secret. Had what happened to you been worse, the decision may have been different… would have been different. 'Fred paused, waiting for Jim to get things straight in his head. He was a good lad, intelligent, but he was still only twelve, Fred was always reminding himself.

'Tom's followed me a few times, well, twice at least, in the last couple of months'. Saying it out loud it sounded like nothing to Jim, but he carried on, wanting to get it out in the open, and to find some reason for the events and Tom's actions. 'He did it to scare me, I know that, but why now, why after so long. He hurt me ' …at this point Jim again felt his arm'… 'Why now?'

Fred paused, and put his arm around the boy's shoulders. He wanted to protect him, but at the same time the lad had to protect himself.

'Just because we agreed to you and Bea keeping it secret, does not mean we did not know. You see the village bully come running out of the wood path grinning, and then a few minutes later find you, with a broken arm with a boot print on it' … at this point he felt Jim shudder…'even an old bugger like me can put two and two together, mores the point, so can the whole village'. He took his arm from around his grandson, and stretched his legs out, giving himself a few seconds to word the next part. 'You heard he is off to join the army? Ever wondered why? Have you ever seen him up the orchard, or on any of the farms you visit with Mr George? People knew, and people did not take kindly to what he did. So he carried on living with his folks, who are good, god fearing people, but no one around here would give him anything. I guess he thought, hoped, that might change with time, but it was a forlorn hope.' Fred paused, and looked at Jim. 'So now he is off to the army, and good riddance. But, I imagine that is why he has decided to bring up the past. He is trying to scare you, but it's only for a few weeks. Just avoid him, and once he has gone life can move on.'

Those final words raised a memory in Jim's head, similar advice being given by the reverend all those years ago. It had not worked then. He looked at his granddad, and could see the concern on the old man's face. He forced a smile.

‘Thank you. I will take care, I promise’. He got up to move, and walked a few paces. ‘I am going out with Peter in a bit, I won’t be late, going up to the bridge and the signal box probably’.

‘Good idea, you take care, and say “Hello” for me to whoever is working in there!’

Jim was already halfway down the garden path, and threw a quick ‘Will do!’ over his shoulder, before disappearing into the house.

Chapter 8

The smell of freshly cooked bread assailed Jim's nostrils as soon as he entered the kitchen.

'Don't you go near it until you have washed those hands! Heaven knows where they have been while you were round and about all those farms this morning. Get and wash them.'

His gran had ordered him, so he quickly moved over to the sink by the window, and turned the tap. As the ice cold water cascaded over his hands, he looked out of the window and down the back garden. His granddad had moved back to the part of the vegetable patch he had been weeding when Jim arrived. As if he could sense being watched, Fred looked up, raised his hand in acknowledgement towards the house, then slowly sank to his knees to carry on his work.

'Weeding my foot! There are a hundred and one jobs I have for him, and he's out there finding himself work to avoid me' Mabel announced, as Jim turned off the tap and dried his hands on an old towel. 'Right, you can cut yourself a slice, then get out of my hair for the afternoon. Your Mum will be back around five, so make sure you are back then'.

Jim nodded his head in acknowledgement, while eating the warm bread as quickly as he could manage. He hadn't realized how hungry he was, until he had smelt the bread minutes earlier, and his stomach had been woken up with a start. Finishing the last mouthful, he gave his gran a quick hug, and walked to the back door, to await his friend's arrival.

Sitting on the back step, in the shade from the sun, he turned over the conversation he had just had with his granddad. Remembering the events at the fayre, it did make sense that people would have worked out what happened. But in his youth, and

Bea's, because no one discussed it, they themselves did not mention it, and the events slowly just vanished into history. And once his arm had healed, he never really thought of it again, until the last couple of months. Maybe his granddad was right; just keep his head, avoid Tom and think of the what he was going to do after school. That was the priority, and that problem would still be there after Tom had gone.

He looked up and saw Peter walking purposely up the road, and got to his feet himself to greet him. He would keep the conversation to himself… their friendship held no boundaries normally, but Jim felt this was something he did not want other people to worry about.

'Heavens its hot!' exclaimed his friend as he opened the latch on the gate and wandered up the path. 'If you suggest football you are on your own!'… Jim laughed, and opened the back door behind him.

'No chance, I'm with you, lets walk up the bridge. If we go through the garden we can walk up the hedgerow and be in the shade for a bit.' He held the door open for his friend and they walked through into the back garden. Fred was still weeding, and looked up as the boys went past.

'Enjoy your afternoon boys' he shouted without looking up.

'See you later, Granddad', and the boys were up and over the fence, and into the field behind.

It was not far short of midsummer, and the boys were in the hot glare of the sun as soon as they entered the field, so they quickly turned to the left to walk up the bridle path to the side of the field. The temperature perceptibly dropped a few degrees as they entered the cover of the hedgerow and trees that ran alongside the field, and they sauntered along, safe in the knowledge it was the one afternoon a week they had nothing to do. The silence was total, this far from the houses and roads, and the field had been left to pasture this year, so no workers were within sight. Jim looked around, and relaxed in the cool and the quiet, the day's anxieties falling off him with each step. The cool was short lived, as they soon reached the end of the field, and were over the stile and into the road.

'Too hot, Jim, lets rest in the oak for a bit?' suggested Peter, as they crossed the road and then turned towards the bridge in the distance. The oak was in the corner of the field that ran up towards the bridge, and without discussion, the boys cut through a gap in the hedge and headed the few yards towards the old tree.

Peter immediately collapsed onto the floor by the trunk with a grunt, arm coming up over his face and as he lay back a sigh escaped from his pursed lips.

'Old Taylors alright, y'know, but that was hard work this morning'. He took his arm from over his eyes and looked at his friend. 'I don't mind the hard work, it's when it's this hot it makes it worse!'

Jim nodded, having worked in the fields and orchards himself at different times.

'It's better when I am working with Mr George… it's hard work on the farms, but between times you can relax a bit in the cart going to the next place'. Jim looked across the field, and then back to his friend. 'You still looking forward to the smithy?' He knew Peter's uncle was a blacksmith in the next town, and the plan was for Peter to move there and work as his apprentice. His parents just did not see the work for him locally, his father being a farm labourer, and there were only so many jobs on the fields. At least he had something to go to, unlike Jim.

'Yeah, my uncles alright, been there a few times, its hard work, but it's a trade'. He slowly sat up and looked back to the village with a sigh. 'There's little for me here, not enough work for the adults, never mind the children like us'. He looked at his friend, to ask the question he had asked many times, and already knew the answer to. 'What are you going to do? Stay around here?' He knew Jim had little choice, but hoped his friend would maybe come with him when he went, find work in the town. His uncle had offered lodgings, but no job. But he knew Jim felt responsible for his mum and grandparents. He knew some part of him felt he was indebted to them, especially since his father left. How could he leave them? Jim looked back at Peter.

'Nothing has changed… I guess I am hoping Mr George will be able to help, if not it will be round the farms, and then Mr Taylor during the summer. Not much else I can do'. A voice inside asked 'And Bea?' He agreed he did also want to stay because of her, but what then? If she did move with the family she worked for down to London, where would that leave him… how sure was he that he wanted to stay… were his family a reason, or an excuse to stay close to Bea. He was not sure, and did not want to investigate the question, in case he was not happy with the answer he found.

'Well..' Peter stated.. 'you know my uncle's offer is still there'. He did not continue, knowing as well as his friend that it was not an offer that was likely to be taken up. 'C'mon, let's get up the bridge, see who us up there. Hopefully Mr Hill is in the signal box, he is always good for a sweet and to let us in for a chat'. With that he purposefully got up, yanked Jim to his feet, and they made their way back towards the road.

The road lead up a slight incline towards the railway track, and had open fields either side, just the odd tree and the hedgerow providing limited shade for the two boys walking alongside the verge.

'We should have stayed under the tree, and slept the afternoon away!' muttered Peter, as their usual quick walk slowly reduced to something not more than a shuffle… the heat of the day and the week's work taking its toll on limbs that were expected to do a man's work, but were still moving throw the growth spurt and growing pains of youth.

'It'll be worth it, Mr Hill will have a couple of sweets, and a glass of water. While we are doing this, at least we are not working' Jim breathed back, though inside he did agree his friend made a good point. However, the brow of the hill was now crested, and around a hundred yards away they could see the bridge in the haze, with the gate to the side leading to a path running down to the signal box. The tracks split here, and again fifty or so yards further along the right spur, and the box was manned all day round, and all year round to Jim's knowledge. Where the lines split, one went north, one south towards London, and the third towards Bristol in the east. It was a busy line, and they had heard two trains speed past since they left the village, barely within earshot but the plume of smoke visible from a distance away.

Energy returned at the sight of the gate. Jim turned to his pal 'Anyway, you're gonna be a blacksmith, you better get used to heat!' He nudged his friend mid walk into the hedge, and jogged off toward the gate.

'Clown, get back here!' came the grunted response, as Peter picked himself up and ran after his assailant. Jim had waited by the gate, smiling, and then turned and led the way down the path that ran fifty yards or so down the gradient towards the signal box. Peter looked at their destination as they walked, a building the size of a two story cottage, the downstairs all walled up, where the machinery was, and the upstairs with three sides consisting mainly of glass, inside which the signalman worked. He quickly looked down at his feet, slipping occasionally on the slim sliver of pathway, and kept his head down until they were yards from the box.

'What are you two vagabonds up to?' came a shout from the upstairs of the building, and both boys looked up to see Mr Hill, a man of medium build, with glasses and receding hair, that at this moment was covered by the cap of a signalman, part of the blue uniform of the men who worked for this railway company.

'Hello Mr Hill, we just came along to see if you needed any help with that tin of sweets you keep hidden away?' suggested Jim.

'Cheeky beggar' exclaimed the railway man as he rubbed his chin, deep in thought. 'Well, you had better come up, just in case…but the 2:30 is due any minute, so if you want any sweets you can do some work first,' and he turned from the window to the upstairs door, opening it as the two boys ran up the metal outside stairs and into the room.

'Over there you go', he ordered as he pointed towards the row of levers, around four foot high running the length of the room. 'Green 4' the shout came, and the boys went and stood by the lever with the green handle and the number four painted on the front. 'When I say' warned Mr Hill, as he walked behind the boys and to the end of the room, looking out of the window. Looking around him, they could both see the curve of the right hand track cut into the landscape, disappearing round the corner. Nothing happened for a few moments, and Jim realized he was holding his breath. He forced himself to stop, and as he did so he saw a small plume of smoke appear above the rise of earth, and at the same time the signalman said 'Now!'

Both boys actuated the lever, one on either side, and pulled it towards them, inch by inch, until it slotted into position, like a cog into a gear. The levers were heavy, but Jim noticed that Mr Hill and walked back behind them while they did it, just in case they needed help. All three looked up, and the train was now starting to pull level with the signal box. Mr Hill was at the window, and Jim saw him and the driver exchange waves, as the train edged past…seven carriages…and then it was past and moving down the line, picking up speed after it had slowed down at the junction.

‘Right, back it goes, you’ve not finished yet’, and the boys repeated the process, pushing the handle back to whence it had come.

‘The 2:45 is the next, on the other track’ explained the signalman. ‘Right, sweets, don’t rightly know that I have any’, and he walked over to a chest of drawers at the back of the room. Opening the top one, he took out around metal tin, taking the lid off and offering one to the boys. ‘I suppose one minute of work is worth a sweet’. Both the youngsters looked in, the tin full of wine gums and aniseed balls, and grabbed one of each, thanking the older man. ‘You’re very welcome, nice to have some company. He turned and put the tin away, asking ‘How’s your granddad Jim?’ as he did so.

‘He is good, thank you Mr Hill. Busy in his garden, and does a bit of fruit picking when he can.’

‘Yes, busy avoiding Mabel it sounds like to me’ replied the signalman with a chuckle. ‘Your granddad’s a wily one. There’s the tap and a couple of mugs, help yourself to some water, you looked like a couple of beetroot faces walking down that path, get some water down you’.

Jim filled a chipped china mug, gulping half of it down after filling it, before offering it to Peter, who emptied the glass.

‘What time do you finish sir?’ he asked as he took the mug to the sink.

‘Six, with luck… six ‘till six. What are you lads up to then, no good I should imagine?’

Jim laughed ‘No work for us today, sir, so granddad told us to go and see a proper workman do his job, so we came to see you!’

The older man laughed, ‘Cheeky bleeder, you won’t have any more sweets for that, so don’t think you will’. He looked at Jim smiling ‘You go back and tell him I told you to go back and watch him in the garden to learn how to be a loafer! Now, the next train is here in a bit, and my boss will be after that, so you had better make a move'. He shooed the boys across the room and back to the door. 'Nice to see you lads' he called after them, as they went back down the stairs, shutting the door behind him.

'What now?' asked Peter, following Jim back up the path. 'It's too hot to do anything'. Jim had been watching his feet as he walked, but looked up to turn around to reply, only for what he saw to stop him in his tracks. Peter, walked into him, slightly losing his footing.

'Hey, what's the game' his friend exclaimed, before he too looked up and saw Tom Smith at the top of the path, a few yards inside the gate.

Jim paused. The air seemed to warm up around him, and any noise disappeared. He looked at Tom, who just stood there, not moving. The options flew through his mind all at once, and none really seemed to provide the solution to the problem. If he turned, and went back to the signal box, it would be like admitting he was scared, but more important to Jim it would be avoiding the problem. And Peter would wonder what was happening. He knew nothing, or so he thought, about the history of the boys. That only left one option, and Jim knew what his course of action would be from the moment the boys stopped walking and saw the figure above. He took a step forward, and carried on, looking at Tom. At the same point, the other boy, man Jim corrected himself, started walking towards him, the distance between them quickly reducing. Barely ten yards separated them, when Tom broke the silence.

'Now Jim, you just walk back, I was on this path first'. Jim knew he had no reason to be here, the path only led to the signal box. It was obvious the boy had followed him, for whatever reason. His granddad's words were still fresh in his head, and all he was focused on was getting past Tom and back on the road home. He had no desire to fight, and knew the other boy was older and bigger. He could hold his own, but what would the point be? Then he thought about the past, and Tom thinking he was being forced to leave by Jim, and for the first time since he set eyes on the boy by the gate, a seed of real fear was felt in the pit of his stomach. Front it out, he thought. The gates not twenty yards away, let Tom show off and make his point, then it's over.

'Just let us past Tom, the gates there, we are due home now', he asked, trying to keep his voice steady and stop the seed from developing further. The other boy smirked, and emitted a grunt as his response. Running his hands through his hair, he feigned considering the request, then looked back at Jim.

'I don't think so, boy. You'e stopped me getting what I want in the past, and now I want to go down this path, so move along, like a good little Jim'. Peter tugged on his friend's arm, but Jim did not turn.

'Come on', he whispered, 'let's just go back, let him past, we will be on the road in a minute'. Unbeknown to Jim, like the rest of the village he did have some knowledge of the past, but primarily he just knew Tom was a bully, and a bitter one at that. Discretion was the best course, until he had deserted the village.

The thought occurred again to Jim, but how many times would this happen? What if he did not leave? What if he came back in future? At what point do you make a stand? He knew Mr Hill would be around, so what was the worst that could happen? A quick fight and it would be over. Jim looked back at Peter, whispered 'No', and then back towards Tom. 'Sorry, Tom, I need to get home', and started walking again up towards the road, never taking his eyes of his adversary.

For a brief second Tom's confidence wavered, it could be seen in his face, then his inbuilt self-belief re-asserted itself, and the boy bellowed 'NO!' as he moved forward, and once within range threw his right fist towards Jim with as much power as he could. The younger boy dodged it, never taking his eyes off Tom, and then the boys were gripped together, the older, slightly taller trying to pummel the younger from higher up the path, punches aimed for his head and shoulders, while Jim had Tom grabbed round the waist and responded with digs into the ribs and back. The gravel moved quickly under their heavy footfalls, and within seconds Tom's feet shot out from under him and he hit the path on his back, the wind knocked out of him. Jim landed on top, throwing a punch that missed the boy who was there a second before, his footing also being lost.

Peter took a quick step or two forward, leaning down and grabbing his friend by the shoulders, trying to yank him up and on to his feet. With a mighty effort he got him a foot up in the air, and Jim pushed down on Tom's chest, and was up on his feet and sliding down the path, spinning round Peter who still had one hand on his shoulder, the other thrown out to the side to keep his balance.

Fury surged through Tom, lain on the path with gravel in his hair, scratches in the palm of his hand and he could even feel where the younger boy had deigned to punch him on his ribs! A boy years younger! Eyes focused on Jim, he leapt to his feet and threw himself bodily towards the young boy, arms outstretched, fingers splayed. Stood side on, Peter saw the body leap on the edge of his vision, and instinctively moved forward, to get between the assailant and his target. His body had gone no more than a foot forward, when his right foot gave way under him, slipping on the gravel and shooting out and up into mid-air. At the moment his mind registered the fact, Tom's hands hit him in the chest, hard his collar bone, spinning him like a top on the edges of the path. One foot in the air, the other now slipped, and after a split second in mid- air, a cry of surprise left his lips, his back hit the embankment with his body tobogganing head first towards the railway line.

Jim now faced the signal box after being picked up bodily by Peter, and felt a body thump onto the floor on his right, just as he heard a cry from his left, that even in his disorientation, he knew was Peter. He looked over towards the sound, just in time to see his friend disappear over the side of the path. 'Peter!' Ignoring his tormentor behind him, he threw himself towards where he had last seen his friend, and his body hit the floor and he stared down the direction the fall had taken his friend. As he focused on the embankment, that was maybe three stories high at this point, he turned his head towards the track, just in time to see Peter's head hit a pile of railway line girders at the bottom of the embankment.

For a moment the world seemed to stop. Disbelief seemed to freeze all of Jim's faculties, as he stared down the embankment at his friend, trying to comprehend what he was seeing. His friend was not moving, and lay at an awkward angle. On the edge of his awareness, he heard the upper door of the signal box crash open, and Mr Hill shout his friend's name, loud enough to bring him to his senses. Jim scrambled to his feet, barely aware of Tom getting to his and staring open mouthed down the embankment, before setting off unsteadily up the path, scrambling to get away from the tragic scene. Sweat still covering his face, along with the detritus from the path picked up during the fight, he set off down the path, slipping and sliding in his haste, arriving at the bottom just as Mr Hill reached the bottom of the steps.

'Jim, wait, stay here.'

He heard the signalman urgently call out to him, while reaching toward him at the same time, but he was round the corner and away down the track, thirty yards or so towards the prone figure, fear driving his legs forward. Jim slowed down momentarily, before throwing himself to his knees alongside his friend.

'Peter!'

No response, and he knew as he shouted the words there would not be any response from his friend again. His face was slowly losing colour already, moving to grey from the flushed face of excitement and energy that had flowed over it just moments earlier. Jim's eyes moved to the left, and saw an ever expanding pool of blood flowing from underneath Peters head. Mr Hill arrived seconds later, kneeling down and resting both hands on his shoulders, just as he looked up at the sky, tears starting to fall down his face, closed his eyes and screamed.

Chapter 9

Jim was sat at Peter's house, in the garden. He was alone. He preferred it that way. No questions. No adults asking if he was alright, or talking in stage whispers when he was around. He just wanted to be alone. The funeral that morning was still a raw scab in his memory, something that he knew he would pick and worry at for a long time, if not forever.

He had stayed with Peter on the day, holding his hand until his friend's parents arrived, and the undertaker. His own mother arrived at the same time, but he would not leave Peter. The adults looked worried, and whispered to each other, but eventually they agreed that he could go back with his dead friend. He could not leave Peter. He had not kept him safe. Tom had been Jim's problem, and now Peter lay dead. Later that night he fell asleep at the undertakers, shock finally taking over his body, as his mother and grandparents took him home, his granddad carrying him slowly back to the house, struggling under the weight.

He woke just as he was lifted into the bed. The night passed slowly. Sleep would not come back at any point, and whenever he did drop off, the events of the day crashed into his thoughts and dreams, bringing him back to reality with jolt. He got up at dawn, the sun starting to beam in through the thin curtains at the window, slowly lighting up the room, although the family still slept, he assumed. Jim quickly got dressed and snuck out of the bedroom, and down the stairs, avoiding through years of practice, the squeaks and groans of certain steps. He had left his boots by the back door, and was out and walking down the road within minutes of first stretching his legs out of the bed.

Walk was the only thing he wanted, fresh air, and to be alone with his thoughts, and his guilt. Not really taking any notice, the sun already warming his back at this early hour, Jim headed towards the next village, the walk he and Peter used to take to school, not really taking any notice or wondering why. Time frustrated him. How could it only be less than eighteen hours since it had happened! Almost a day, but the event that had taken his best friend's life had taken just a few seconds. His friend was gone, he himself would never be the same. Peter's family, he knew, were distraught. The whole village seemed sombre. He could not remember a death in the village, certainly not anyone so young.

Why had he not just turned and walked away? What did an argument on a path mean? Nothing. So why had he acted like he did? It was Tom who started it, that was where the fault lay, Jim knew that, but he could have stopped it… he could have made a different decision. Looking up, he saw he was past the Manor House. Sunday, and the world was silent for one day. But there was church today. The thought made Jim feel sick. He wanted to go, that was what people did at times like this. Religion was there to support, and nurture and guide. But what about the people? How would they look at him? Jim had left the house needing space, and time to be alone, now he wanted his family. He turned, and ran back down the road back towards home. Faster and faster, the sweat that was running down his face, fuelled by the physical effort he was expending joined by the warmth of the sun, was soon mingling with tears, as his vision started to blur long before he reached home.

He spent the day there. Jim's mum and grandparents wanted him to go to church, but the thought of all those people just scared him.

'You are not to blame, Jim, it was just an accident. People know that. It's not your fault. The longer you take coming back out into the world the harder it will be' his Granddad cajoled.

He could not face it, despite knowing in his heart it was the right thing to do. He just wanted to get this day out of the way. Just one day. He would just sit and read, or do some work in the garden.

Just don't let me see anyone, he thought. Just leave me alone. People came to see him, he heard them talking to his mum on the doorstep, or his granddad in the road. Offering condolences, asking after him … 'wasn't it a shame,'.. 'terrible accident,'… 'such a lovely boy, Tom's not been seen since.' The words meant nothing, did not change anything. His friend was dead. Nothing would bring him back. And he could have stopped it.

The following days all merged into one, prior to the funeral that was on the Wednesday. People asking, cajoling, trying to get him to speak about what had happened. But what was the point? It would not change anything. A policeman from the next town came, but he had little interest, there was nothing untoward in his eyes, it was simply an awful accident. His advice amounted to 'getting on with life, men don't cry'. Jim did listen to him, you respected the police. But he still felt hollow, he felt guilty. And he wanted to feel the guilt, he wanted to feel the pain.

The funeral was his first, he had never been to one before. It seemed like almost the whole village was there, everyone in their Sunday best. He was close to the front, and just stared at the coffin. During the eulogy, the only sound you could hear was Peter's mother crying. Sobbing. Outside afterwards, he joined the others in throwing some soil on the coffin in the grave, taking his turn with the other mourners. But still the emptiness was there. Still the guilt. He had not cried yet. People said it was strange, he should talk, he should cry, he should do this, he should do that. He just felt nothing, apart from the feeling that came with knowing it was his fault. Leaving the graveyard, he walked past Peter's father. He shook Jim's hand, and put his other hand on Jim's shoulder.

'Don't worry, it'll be OK' he whispered, and offered a faint smile.

Jim moved on, and offered his condolences to Peter's mother. But she did not reply, would not even look him in the eye. Just stared down the line. He moved on, understanding but hurt at the same time. His granddad put his arm around him, they walked down the lane, onto the road and down to the village for the wake, a long grey line of human misery streaming out of the church.

After the drinks in the house, the adults began to talk, the strictures of the day slowly easing, as people tried to find their way back into normality. Jim even heard the odd laugh, conversation about work, the weather, and took his chance to move into the garden and the peace and quiet. Lost in his reverie, he only noticed someone was sitting down beside him at the last minute. Looking to his side, Reverend Steed looked back at him.

'Hello Jim. I saw you come out here. I imagine you feel the same as I at these occasions? This morning we are in mourning and in deep sorrow, tomorrow is a new day. This afternoon, we are changing, neither one nor the other. It's a difficult time'.

Jim nodded, and looked back down the garden, watching some younger children form the village playing.

'We all cope and change in different ways' continued the curate, seemingly reading Jim's mind. 'Those youngsters will be quick, in a day or so they will forget, and it will only come back as a feint memory in years to come. Older villagers, like myself, have seen an awful lot of death. You never get used to it, but you find a way to cope, a mechanism if you like, and you use it to move forward with your life'.

He sighed, his voice lowering. He put his hand on the youngsters shoulder, and looked at his young companion.

'It's harder for people of your age… enough experience to know what has happened and be deeply hurt, but not enough to know what to do about it. It takes time. The trick is not to rush forward too quickly. Do what feels right in here' …the old man touched his chest with his other hand…' as much as here' … and moved it to rest gently on his head. 'I am sure you have lots of advice, and people telling you what to do, and what not to do. The most important person to listen to is yourself.' He squeezed Jim's shoulder and slowly got to his feet. 'You have your whole life ahead, Jim. It's not important how quickly you grieve and move on, only that you do. Peter will always be in your heart, that's all that matters'.

The old man moved away, pausing briefly to watch the children play for a moment, then smiled and moved back into the house, intent on passing on his condolences and leaving the family to have some time to themselves. It was very true what I told Jim, he thought as he moved up the back steps. We do cope. He looked up and saw Peter's mother at the top of the steps. But it certainly does not make it any easier, he thought, as he moved to embrace the distraught parent.

Chapter 10

The school gates opened, and the children flooded out into the road, lanes and fields. All ages were covered, as they went their own separate ways. The younger ones disappeared home, to play alone or with friends, the older ones to do chores with a hope of seeing friends later. School was over for the summer, and for the older children it was over for good. Jim was one of the last to leave, along with around fifteen other children the same age. School had been a constant in his life up until this point, but now it was over. He paused at the gates, watching bodies scatter in every direction, and paused to take it in. This would be his last day. Now, he needed to be a man, for his mother, and for his grandparents. Mostly for himself, he thought. The last few weeks had been cold and lonely. Isolated. It was not the fault of anyone. Family, friends and villagers all tried to talk, and life seemingly carried on as normal in the outside world. But to Jim, he felt like an actor. Saying the right things, responding how he was expected to, going through the motions. He even had short periods when he felt like himself again, but no sooner had realization emerged than the image of his dead friend came into his head, and the thoughts and memories of that day came back into the foreground of his mind.

'Fancy walking a young lady home, stranger?'

The words shocked Jim out of his thoughts, and he turned to see Bea stood behind him.

'Not just you children who are finished, that's me done as well until next term'. He saw her pinning her long black hair into a bun behind her head, before adorning herself with a cloche hat. She looked at him and winked, putting her hand onto the inside of his elbow. 'Come on Mr Turner, stop gawking at me, I am working at the manor house in half an hour, so you have got that long to brighten my day'.

Jim smiled, accepting her hand on his arm and walked slowly round the corner towards the road, both of them a similar height, their strides matching. This is what was comfortable about Bea, he thought, probably for the umpteenth time. She just spoke to him with honestly and openness, in many ways like his granddad. Everyone else seemed to be dancing around him, either avoiding the subject of Peter altogether, so that it became a shadow over every conversation, or doing the opposite, and looking at him with tears in their eyes, as if trying to force the grief out of him that he would not show. Bea spoke to him like she had always done.

They walked in silence for a while, the tensions in Jim's shoulders slowly dissipating with every step. Bea let the silence meander as they walked, then broke it when she felt Jim was comfortable.

'Do you think you will miss it? I know everyone says they hate it, me too, it's not that many years since I left!' Jim looked ahead, thinking about the answer, then looked sideways at his friend.

'Yes. I will. Some parts were horrible, but I enjoyed learning, and the routine. And getting to spend time with my pals every day'. His voice tailed off, and his eyes slid down to the floor as they continued walking. Bea let the silence settle again. They had passed a row of cottages, and saw some of the younger children in the garden, who had lost no time in running home as soon as the bell was rung. She saw his eyes, wander towards them, and then back to the floor.

'You must miss Peter?' The question hung for a second.

'Yes. Every day'. She saw a tear emerge and make its way down his cheek, so she looked ahead and chose to ignore it, knowing it was not something a boy would want to be drawing attention to, no matter how unhappy he was.

‘That’s not a bad thing. I liked Peter. Everyone did. You don’t want to forget the people who mean a lot to you’. He left the tear, either unaware or unable to bring himself to wipe it away.

‘But it’s my fault. I miss him and it’s my fault. I did this. It was me!’

The last few words came out as a sob, but still he would not let himself stop, still he kept walking, as the tears rolled down his face. Bea continued, caught in the moment and aware they were now in the countryside, halfway between the school and the manor house.

‘Why was it your fault?’ She held on to his arm slightly tighter, letting him know she was there. A few paces passed, as Jim tried to control his emotions, and his breathing. He wanted to talk, wanted to explain his feelings, it had been bottled up inside him for weeks, but this was Bea, his friend, but also someone he thought he probably had deeper feelings for. It was right, but it also felt wrong at the same time.

‘I could have walked away, but I didn’t. Tom was looking for a fight. I knew it. I could have just turned and gone, Peter even said so. It was my pride, after what Tom did to you that time, and what he did to my arm.’ He walked a few steps more, then stopped and turned to face Bea. ‘My pride killed my best friend.’

There were no new tears left to fall, old ones drying on his face. As Bea looked at him, she could see at the same time, layer on layer, the small boy who stood up for her, the grown up boy before her, and the man he would become in years to come.

She turned, and walked to a field gate just behind them, looking up and seeing they were not a hundred yards from the drive leading to the Manor House. She leant and sat on the bar, Jim following and sitting alongside her, all emotion spent, shoulders slumped. She composed her thoughts, then looked at her friend.

'You can't change the past, as much we all want to at times. What's happened has happened. And anything you do will always be a part of you. But you have to stop thinking your pride killed Peter. It was an accident, a million to one chance. It is horrible. But don't think one decision caused it. There are hundreds of things that happened that day alone, changing any one of them could have changed the outcome. And not just that day, on other days'.

She quietly changed position, to be more comfortable, aware she needed to be at work but also aware it was important to talk to Jim at this moment, a chance that may not come again soon.

'You can take it as far back as you can, to the day you stopped Tom in the orchard. That day you stood up for yourself and me, and I will be forever grateful, and love you for it. You did the right thing that day, and should be proud, and you did the right thing by the signal box. It was just a horrible accident'.

She stopped, worried if her words were right, she was barely seventeen, and trying to support and help a boy who was blaming himself for the death of his friend. Bea opened her mouth to say more, then closed it again. They sat in silence for a few moments, before Jim finally looked up.

'I think we had better walk you to work', and stood up and waited while Bea smoothed her dress down and stretched her legs.

They moved back towards the road, walking along the hedgerow towards the Manor House drive, both deep in their own thoughts. The walk only took a few minutes, and soon the pair were at the back servants' entrance to the house. Bea straightened herself out, for the final time, and thanked Jim for walking her to work. She turned and put her hand on the door, as Jim said 'Bea!'… making her turn quickly. She took in the face, and realized the boy she had seen earlier was gone, and the man he would become was coming to the surface. He physically straightened as she looked, and a sad smile crept across his face.

‘Thank you for talking. I…I think, well, it helped, and it will help. I like talking to you’. The last followed by a red flush spreading across his face from his ruddy cheekbones.

‘Well I enjoy talking to you Jim Turner’, responded Bea, giving a short curtsey, ‘you take care. You’re a good person’, and she turned and entered the house, closing the door behind her.

Jim stood for a moment, then moved back toward the drive and up towards the road. He thought about what Bea had said, and the Reverend as well. He was so deep in thought, he did not respond when, on two occasions, passing horse and cart drivers would shout acknowledgement. The hurt would always be there, he decided. It would not go, it would always be hiding in the pit of his stomach, smaller some days, larger others but always there. But it was a part of him, and he would live with it. Or try to. He turned into the village and up towards his parents, his mind turning to the next afternoon, day, weeks and months. School had just finished, and although he still had numerous odd jobs, he needed to decide what he was going to do. It made him think of Bea, taking her to work, and the possibility she may move to London. His mind wandered to the conversation they had, not twenty minutes before. And as he put his hand on the back door handle, with the sound of his Granddad’s voice on the other side, a frown creased his brow, but for the first time in a very long time he felt a weight had been lifted.

Chapter 11

The following days and weeks brought a routine of sorts to Jim's life, but without ever solving the problem of what he was to do with that life. The mornings of that long, hot summer were spent with Mr George, the vet. He thought that when he would look back in later life, his summer would consist of being sat on the horse and cart with the older man, moving from farm to farm and village to village. The lanes and tracks between the farms and villages meandered across the countryside, moving through farmland busy with workers getting crops in, through the quiet, cool woods to the north of the area, from sunlight to shade. This time, between jobs, was the most fruitful time for the young man. Invariably, the early part of the journey would involve talking about what they had both just seen and done, the veterinary explaining to Jim what had happened and why he had chosen the course of action he had, all the time explaining that the profession was still in its infancy. He rarely failed at some point each day to pronounce that he never stopped learning about the animals and their ailments, as well as the owners and their idiosyncrasies.

After they had dissected the latest events, they would invariably fall into silence, as Bill George focused on driving the trap, and Jim was content with his own thoughts. He used this time to mull over the events of the past few months, slowly coming to terms with them, and his life now. As they drove down the lane, trees either side of the road and the rays of the sun breaking through the canopy of leaves and branches above, he slowly came to an acceptance of what had happened and his part in it. The journeys and musings on the trap, building on the groundwork started by the conversation with Bea on the day he left school.

His thoughts turned to Bea, not for the first time that day. He had seen little of her in the weeks since that day. He was working as much as he could, and when not working was helping at home. He knew she was working full time at the Manor House now that school had finished, and had only caught a glimpse of her a couple of times since, a raised hand in acknowledgment across a distance all he could manage. He knew he wanted to see her, if only to thank her, but they never seemed to cross each other's paths. And the thought of that one word she had said about love scared him as much as excited him, to the point he felt torn in two directions, wanting desperately to see her, but scared that he was placing more weight on that one word that he should, the fear of rejection and embarrassment stopping him from seeking her out, adding to his confusion.

They had one more call that morning, an ailing cow on one of the furthest farms from the village, that Bill George treated with his usual mix of potions, dependent on beast and problem, and Jim was just a fetcher and carrier while on the farm. He still watched and listened, desperate to eek out any knowledge he could from every event, the possibility of this as a job still very much alive in his mind. They had left after twenty minutes, and started the journey back.

'You in the orchard again today, Jim?'

'Yes, I think Mr Taylor still wants me, and if not I will see if anything needs doing in the churchyard.'

He looked across the fields they were passing into the distance, his eyes seemingly focused on the horizon, but his thoughts most obviously elsewhere. Bill George looked at him, and offered a knowing smile as he turned to give his full attention back to the road. You had to give the lad his due, he worked harder than most, and wanted to learn every day. His eyes softened and his face appeared downcast, as he thought for all his effort, a place like this held little promise for the young.

The afternoon's work was steady in the orchard, Jim doing the fetching and carrying his friend had been doing all those months before. There was little time for thought and even less for any chatter between the workers, the heat pleasant on his face in the late summer sun. Slowly the pickers left towards the end of the afternoon, and he finished the last round before leaving himself, and taking the footpath from the orchard back to the village. For once, this was not taken at a trot or sprint, as he took the moment to relax and enjoy the solitude. Feet plodded one to the other, the day's work in the sun even taking its toll on someone so young. Jim noticed his thoughts turn to Bea, as they invariably did any moment his mind was not occupied. Coming towards the end of the path, he looked up from his feet, and there she stood, by the gate, as if the intensity of his thoughts had brought her to this place. He could feel his cheeks start to redden, as if Bea may have been able to read his thoughts… she must have been watching him walk down from the orchard, waiting for his arrival.

'Could you walk any slower?! I thought you were usually running everywhere….like waiting for Christmas that was. ' she said sarcastically but with a supportive smile. Bea was wearing the same clothes she did on the day after school, he noticed. Why did he remember that?

'Sorry, its tiring today, my Mum is always saying I should slow down'.

'I'm only joking, am in no rush. Do you need to get home, I fancied a quick chat?' A slight unease crept up on Jim. Not knowing why, he pushed the feeling down and chose to ignore it, for now.

'Yep, Mum's at work, no rush. How are you? I haven't see you for a while, are you OK?' He knew he was gabbling, and Bea laughed in response.

'One question at a time!' She sat on the gate and indicated he come up beside her. Even this was fraught with danger for him, sit close, but not too close. Luckily she seemed oblivious to his indecision, but the unease would not leave him completely.

'How's Mr George? I have not seen him for weeks, not since he came and helped us with King.' King was Bea's spaniel, and Jim remembered the day he had been round with the vet to help the dog the previous summer.

'He's good, really helpful, I enjoy it with him. I'd like to work for him, but he has not got the money for me full time'. Jim frowned and looked at his friend. 'I guess I am still deciding what to do'.

'Well, you need to do what you are good at, that's all I can say, really. Something will come along. Keep helping him'. They both looked away, into the distance. 'And in answer to your question, I am very well thank you. But do have some news'. Jim looked back, unease growing again. 'I might as well just say it. I am leaving, going down to London. Mr Carmichael at Manor House is moving to London for his work in the city, and wants the family there with him. They will just keep the manor house for some weekends and holidays. He has asked me to go with them! I was always hoping, and, well, now it has happened'.

Jim looked away. Confusion reigned in his mind, and showed on his face. He knew this was what Bea wanted, and always knew this would most likely happen. But she was such a part of his life and always had been. Right back to the day by the church in the orchard with Tom, up to the walk the day he left school. And he did have feelings for her. Strong feelings that he did not completely understand. He would miss her. After Peter it felt like he was being left alone again.

'I know you have had a hard time this year, with Peter. I don't want you to feel abandoned by me'. He looked back at her.

He wanted her to be happy. This is what she wanted, always had done. He had to be happy for her.

'I think it will be great. You have always talked about this, so I think its fantastic news'. He forced a smile on his lips, fearing it would look more like a grimace. He put his hand on hers. 'Honestly, I am happy for you. When do you go?' Her eyes brightened as returned his gaze.

'In two weeks. Mr and Mrs Carmichael are going, then I follow with the children the following week'. He could hear her voice raise a pitch, and her eyes seemed to brighten as the excitement she felt started to make itself known. 'I can't wait, Jim. Apart from you, there is nothing here. In London there is opportunity, the pay will be better, more people, just a huge city full of life!' At this he knew he had been right to be happy. The joy was evident, as if she glowed.

'I really am pleased, it's a new life for you'. Bea took her hand from under his, and clasped his between both of hers.

'We will always be there for each other Jim. I will come back in summer, we will see each other'. The smile re-appeared. 'But, oh, I can't wait, I really can't!'

Jim was caught up in his friend's obvious joy, and felt infected by it himself. You spoke to anyone around here, and he knew himself, it was a hard life in the agricultural area they lived, with little opportunity. Bea had got a chance to move away, and see what options that in turn opened up in her life. It was good news. But he knew when she left he would not feel it.

'Come on', she interrupted his thoughts, 'Let's go, I need to be places if you don't.' She spun on top of the gate and jumped down with Jim following after, and made their way the short distance to the village, Bea talking all the way about her new life. They parted in the village centre, Jim having barely spoken, and went their own separate ways home, their emotions at either end of the scale.

Chapter 12

The march had stopped, at a meeting point just south of the next town. The men were dismissed, and scattered around the close vicinity, looking for food, somewhere to sleep. The road just a few minutes earlier had been crammed with a long, snaking line of soldiers, and was now deserted, save for a few carts of equipment being pulled by horses. It was afternoon, and the mess tent at this meeting point was the target for the majority of men, Jim amongst them. Taking his turn in the queue, he collected food in his mess tin, then made his way to a sloping hillside along the line of tents with some of his mates from the battalion. Scanning the horizon as he sat and ate, he could see in the horizon where the front line was marked, and the support a mile or so before that. This would be the last moment of relative peace for the coming weeks, and the atmosphere amongst the men had changed from the relaxed time behind the lines that had fuelled the conversation and songs at the start of the walk to the more sullen silence now.

Slowly eating his meagre rations, Jim thought back to the village earlier, and the memories it un-earthed of his early life at home. The reason was clear, the last few weeks he had met up with Bea. The one constant in his life from that time, gone for a fair few months but now back. He had seen her in the field hospital, and they had managed to get a couple of hours together over the course of a day or two, until the last night when he had managed to commandeer a room in a house for them both. It already seemed like weeks ago, but the light she had brought into his life again on seeing her could not be mistaken. It had surprised him, to an extent, and now the deep longing he had in his heart that he could feel in the pit of his stomach made him realize how much he had missed her. And, to an extent, his old life.

Hearing shouting and laughter to his left, Jim turned as he ate his last mouthful, and saw in the next field some of the men playing football. He had seen men kicking a ball ahead as they went over the top, and was still not sure if it was lunacy or good psychology, giving the men something normal to focus on as they did the most abnormal thing under orders. The game appeared to have no rules, just a group of soldiers enjoying the laughter and fun of being out in the open and safe, one last time. Nothing like the football games of his youth, and the actions that made him wince with the memory.

Way after dark that night, Jim was in one of the huge tents that had been put up for the men waiting to go into the support line. There were maybe twenty men in there, and the various grunts, snores and wheezes told him the majority of them were asleep. He rolled onto his back and stared at the roof of the tent. His mind had been wandering back to his youth. He had not thought of those times for years, in fact to a certain extent had blocked them from his memory, with later events the obvious cause. He had not seen his dad since around that time, maybe a few months after he broke his arm… no, after he had had his arm broken for him, he corrected himself. Tom Smith. Could events have turned out differently… could he have done anything differently? But he did not want to think about Tom or that.

His thoughts remained with Bea. She had been a focal point in his life, along with his family, all these years. She had obviously seen something in him all those years ago, whatever that was, and he did not know himself. The vicar too, was a support, right to the end. Jim turned over again, and close by heard the sound of the small steam engines running on the track. These were being used more and more to bring the equipment needed to the front line. They crossed the countryside, moving goods from location to location, before being taken by hand or cart to where they were needed. Jim closed his eyes and soon fell sleep, the low sound of the engine running along the tracks accompanying him to sleep.

Jim opened his eyes. They had been in the front line a few days now, and already the time behind lines seemed like distant memory, something that almost seemed like it had not really happened. Two days before, the march to the front line had continued. The men slogged on down the final few miles. All Jim could see was the back of the man in front, head down. The rain sheeted down, and after five or six rows ahead the figures became a blur. Scarred fields either side, mud the like of which even as a boy brought up in the countryside he had never seen before. A battlefield fought over once, twice. He briefly looked up at the sky, at the dark, low, grey blanket above them, and wondered again how so much had changed so quickly.

A nudge on the shoulder woke him, and he looked up to see his pal Archie slump down beside him. Wide awake already, never properly sleeping in the trench, he grabbed at the tea being offered and warmed his hands. The odd spot of rain dripped from the sky in the darkness.

'What time is it, Arch?'

'Five, or thereabouts. Good dreams?' Jim just smiled in response, and clutched his tin mug tighter. 'Hurry up and drink that, be getting our drop of rum soon, make sure we are ready to go'.

'Jesus'.

The profanity slipped from Jim's mouth, and he mentally apologised to Reverend Steed. Sipping his tea, he looked around, seeing the same activity going on in the parts of the trench that were visible to him. Men sleeping, making tea, nibbling chocolate, lighting a woodbine. The calm before the storm. Or the calm before the slaughter. He finished his tea and stood stretching his legs, the warmth of the dream slowly ebbing away, ushered away by the dark reality that now surrounded him.

The next half an hour was spent checking his equipment, and preparing for what was to come. The general chatter around him slowly dissipated, as the nerves and fear grew with each minute. Jim spent the time by Archie, offering each other support and solace in the heavy atmosphere.

Silence descended, just the soft mutterings of his colleagues up and down the line. Suddenly, as if waiting for a signal, the barrage started. Men hunkered down, used to the noise, or so they thought, but instinct making them draw in on themselves, making themselves smaller if that were possible. Jim drew his collar up, and sat with his back against the corner of the trench, Archie alongside him and men further along the line all taking the same action in various forms. He looked up at the sky, still dark, the rain falling as a light drizzle. Nothing to do but endure. The noise and the fear.

The Captain and the Sergeant came along the line, giving and asking the men to pass on the same message given the previous night. They were going over the top at 6. Jim and Archie had done this before, but the fear did not lessen, the churn in the stomach did not recede. The bombardment stopped as the men made their way along the line, the sergeant giving out a tot of rum to each man.

'Good Man, Jim… give 'em what for… see you on the other side!'

Jim slugged the alcohol back, briefly burning his throat as it went down. He turned and faced the ladder.

'Keep your head down, let's just get back in one piece…. If we can'.

He looked at Archie as his friend spoke and could see his own fear reflected is his friends face, as the rain got heavier.

'Ready….'

Silence…..then the sound of a whistle blast from close behind that seemed to echo down the trench to either side, and Jim found his feet taking him up the ladder and over the top of the trench, a roar erupting from his throat as he went forward, using it to try and drive himself forward into a place he did not want to go. He slipped on emerging from the trench, found his feet quickly, and stumbled forward. He felt Archie's hand on his arm, stopping him from falling. Knowing his friend was just to his side, he moved towards the enemy lines, one small figure in a waves of bodies either side flooding out of the earth.

Machine gun fire started almost immediately, and figures ahead and behind fell to the ground in a heap, as if they were marionettes who were being taken forward by some invisible hand, who had then indeterminately started to cut the strings. In his peripheral vision, Jim saw his Sergeant fall, who had not moments before given him a thimbleful of brandy and spoken to him, and now lay with is life ebbing away. Turning away he spotted Archie a few feet in front, and on the edge of one of the multitude of craters dotted across the deserted land, half full of stinking water and bodies that either side had been unable to reach. He turned slightly to move towards him, thinking the crater may offer some shelter from the inexorable hail of fire they found themselves running towards.

'Archie!'

He knew in the chaos his friend would not hear, but still he shouted, getting slightly closer as a small patch of land hardened almost miraculously under his feet, feet away now with the crater alongside them.

'Archie!'

His friend turned, and as he did so Jim saw the side of his face explode out, the bullet seemingly entering one side and exiting the other almost simultaneously. Archie's legs gave out under him as his fell to the floor and slid over the edge of the crater.

'NOOOO!'

Jim screamed, the noise immediately cut short as he felt what seemed like a hot knife slice into his thigh.

Chapter 13

Jim grimaced. Sweat poured down his brow, as he strained to get his hands hooked round the front hooves of the lamb, the last one of three still inside the mother. He had been on the farm with Bill George for the past couple of hours, and while there, this ewe had started to have difficulty giving birth, the three lambs inside a tangle of legs that could not sort themselves out on their own. With the farmers grudging permission, himself busy with a barn full of ewes soon to be mothers, Jim had set about the task of sorting one leg from the other, and delivering three healthy lambs. Bill was watching on, giving gentle suggestions where needed, and Jim felt sure he could feel the intense stare of the farmer on his back, even though he knew he was otherwise engaged at the other end of the barn at that point. He knew how loathe farmers were to have vets do a job that they invariably felt they could do themselves, and not have to pay for the privilege.

Finally he succeeded in getting the final two small front hooves in position and out into the open air, then delved back in to grab the lamb by the nostrils, and bring it bodily onto the hay covered barnyard floor. The mother exhausted at this point, just looking round at her baby, as Jim cleared the mucus and afterbirth from round the head, face and nostrils. Happy that the lamb was alive, he let Bill pick it up and take it to the other end of the barn, while he did the best he could to wash his arms down with a bucket of cold water, and what was left of any clean straw he could see. He looked up to see his mentor put the lamb in the pen where a ewe with only one lamb could mother it and bring it up. A sense of relief and pride enveloped him, especially when the farmer offered a grunted ‘Well done, lad’ on his way past, the only positive or constructive words he had heard from the man, in the six years he had been working with Bill since he left school.

Jim smiled, and picked up his jacket to make his way back toward the cart they still used. Mr George had still to be convinced he needed a car, as much as Jim tried to convince him a Wolseley, or maybe a new Ford from Manchester would help their business. But he would keep trying, seeing as only the young sometimes see, the change in the world around him since he was a small boy. Still, it was the cart for now, and Jim had to agree on the lanes and tracks they covered, it was probably just as quick as a car, and certainly less liable to break down!

'Good work, lad', complimented Bill as he climbed up on the trap alongside Jim. 'They can always be nasty jobs, and likely as not the last ones dead before it comes out. Happy work this time, but it's not always the case'.

They exited the farm gate, and turned along the road toward the village, the sun low in the sky behind them as the warm late spring day drew to a close.

'He even complimented me!' Jim gave a look of shock at the older man, who laughed loudly, a laugh fuelled by the knowledge that the work of the day was behind him and a quiet evening in the cottage beckoned.

'Don't give me that, you'll be telling me he paid his bill on time next!' Bill glanced at his companion. 'Guess you want to be getting home early, and off up to the Manor House before its dark?' He was greeted in reply with a satisfied smile, as no other response was needed.

Jim's thoughts turned to Bea as they meandered down the lanes back towards the village. The six years since she had left had been both the best of times and the worst of times, Jim thought, the line from the book he was reading fresh in his memory. Bea had flourished in London, enjoying her work, thriving with everything that London had to offer, seeing as much as she could, and as far as her finances allowed. And each year she came back, spring and summer, for a few weeks with the family, back to the manor house. And the close friendship of the early years of their life had flourished. When they were apart, the letters sped to and from London, when money allowed. And then when Bea was here, they spent as much time together as they could. As much as their time together was wonderful, and their relationship as strong as it would ever be, he still found it very frustrating being apart.

He sighed, seeing no end in sight. Bea's life seemed set up for her, but he saw no way to be a part of it all the time. There was nothing he could offer in London, or any way to save the money to take him there… there was little that he could see he could offer in the capital, a young man with knowledge of agriculture, and just starting out, he hoped, on a career as a veterinary. And there was the crux of the problem. It was what he wanted to do, he enjoyed it and felt he had the ability, Bill George was convinced of it. But that was not enough. He should go to college and study it, the Veterinary College in Liverpool was just setting up, but he did not have the money to go there, and neither did his family. Jim's mother was working still, but his grandparents were not, the four of them relying on two lots of wages only, plus whatever vegetables his granddad could sell! No, there was no point worrying at the problem constantly like dog with a bone, he had to accept this was his life. Learn what he could from Bill, with the plan to eventually take on the business entirely, not that the older man looked remotely like giving up, and neither should he.

'You're away with the fairies, lad, penny for them?'

Jim was pulled from his thoughts by the man in question, as they pulled alongside the village pub. He looked across and gave a wan smile.

'Just thinking, Bill'.

'You want to give up on that for a start, no good for anyone! See you in the morning'.

Jim jumped off the cart, and headed into the village towards his grandparent's home, feet shuffling, the thoughts he was mulling over crowding back into his mind with each step.

'God in heaven, you stink!'

His granddad's subtlety never changing, as Jim walked in the back door. The older man moved towards the back door into the garden as Jim came in from the front.

'Get in that bath, and try to leave the contents of the farmyard behind next time you leave it' he chuckled, quickly closing the door behind him.

'Ignore the old bugger' came his Gran's voice from the kitchen 'I've filled the tin bath in the front room, get yourself in it and give us those clothes, tea'll be ready soon'.

'Thanks Gran, you're a savior!' He breathed, as he ran past her in the kitchen, discarding clothes as he went, before disappearing into the room beyond.

'Dearie me, Fred did have a point' she exclaimed, her nose and face wrinkling as she collected the trail of clothes left in the kitchen, the distaste evident, but not so bad that it would stop her doing all she could to keep her grandson looking as clean and smart as possible.

Jim walked back into the kitchen half an hour later, his best clothes on, ready to go and collect Bea from work, just as his mother entered the room from the other end. She smiled as she saw him, but he noticed, not for the first time, how she had aged the last few years. The young face of her youth had gone, and lines had developed, along with dark shadows under her eyes. The smile was a second too late to prevent him from seeing the face of a woman twenty years older.

‘Hello Jim, good day today?’

It hurt him to see her make the effort to physically straighten up and purposefully walk quickly across the small kitchen to the table, when all she really wanted to do was go to bed and fall into a sleep fueled by fatigue. Years of making ends meet and working numerous jobs round the village to help keep the four adults afloat was etched across every line on her face. Again, the guilt he felt that was never far from the surface broke like a wave on a beach, smothering his upbeat mood around the upcoming evening.

‘It went well, spent a lot of the afternoon on the Brookland Farm. Helped deliver some triplets the ewe was struggling with, hard work, but I’m pleased I did it well’.

‘It smelt like hard work, that’s for sure!’ butted in Fred, ’Heaven knows why you have to bring the whole farm back with you!’

Jim laughed, ’If I did not, what would you have to moan about?’ His granddad murmured a reply, as the food was served up by Mabel. The talk tailed away, as the food was eaten, while Jim’s mind wandered to the night ahead.

‘You taking Bea to the pub later, lad? Just asking, don’t want to be no gooseberry to you two love birds.’ Fred was obviously in the mood to prod and poke his grandson, knowing how he felt about Bea.

‘I might, as long as I don’t have to walk you home again’. The barb hit home, and Fred went quiet, as he remembered the night only a month or so before when he had enjoyed the hospitality too long, and Jim had been cajoled into carrying his granddad home when the old man had drunk more than his share. Fred turned to look at his wife, whose returned stare told him to keep quiet and eat his meal, without uttering a word. Jim smiled, finishing his food as quickly as decency would allow.

'Thanks Gran, that was lovely as always' he announced, getting up to take his plate to the sink, and kissing the women of the family on his way back. 'I won't be late, might see you later granddad', and with that he collected his coat and was out through the back door. As soon as he was gone, Mabel looked at her daughter, concern etched on her face.

'You look dreadful, girl, I hope you're not working tomorrow in that state?'

'I am sure I will be fine, Mum, just tired. A good night's sleep and a cuppa in the morning will set me straight'. The faint smile passed over her lips, as she turned back to her food, neither woman convinced by her answer, and neither willing to take the conversation any further.

The night was dark by the time Jim got outside, and he wasted no time in covering the distance to the Manor House. Ringing the bell by the back door, he took a step back, and waited. He felt the usual butterflies in his stomach, the mixture of excitement at seeing her, but also the fear that there would not be many occasions like this before Bea left again for London.

The door squeaked as it was opened, and Bea appeared. Her long black hair was tied up, and covered by a wide brimmed hat, a white blouse was under her dark, waist length jacket, and a long, dark red ankle length skirt. Jim thought she looked stunning. For a moment, he just looked at her, not sure what to say.

'Stop gawping at me, have I spilt something, I was in a rush to get out!' Bea started checking her clothes as she stood in the pale light of the doorway.

'No, no, sorry, you look fine, I mean, sorry, you look beautiful!' She looked up and a smile seemed to start in her eyes and spread across her face as she looked up at him.

'Well, thank you, kind sir! Best compliment I have had since the last one you gave me!' She walked forward and took the crook of his arm that he offered, kissing him on the cheek as she did so. 'Shall we have a drink in the village, in the snug at the pub? Just one, I am shattered'.

'Yes, I was going to ask if that was alright with you, but let's just avoid my Granddad, he is in one of his mischievous moods!' He led the way up the drive, and back towards the village, the lights of the houses on the edge just visible in the darkness.

It was fully dark when they got to the pub, the sky clear and starlit. The snug was empty, so they were glad to have the room to themselves, though Jim thought he could hear his granddad's voice holding court in the bar. He got a beer for himself, poured out of a huge jug by the barman, and a smaller glass for Bea, and went to sit by the smoldering fire, the barman coming over and throwing a log on with a grunt as Jim sat down. Bea had taken off her hat and let her hair down, accepting the drink with a smile and taking a sip.

'I meant it, Bea, you look stunning tonight', a slight flush surfacing on his cheeks, but hidden by the dim light in the heavy beamed room.

'Thank you. You're not too bad yourself', her hand crossing the table to rest on his. 'It's nice to get noticed, after spending each day teaching and playing with children. I would wear a hessian sack and they would not notice or care'. She took another sip, and settled back on the chair, enjoying the warmth of the crackling fire and the peace and quiet, just the slight hubbub from the neighbouring room letting them know they were not completely alone.

She looked at Jim, mulling over, as she had done at various times all day, the best and safest route to bring the subject up that had been resting in the corner of her mind for months, growing each day and seeking an audience. Unaware of doing it, she slightly bit her upper lip, and asked him how work was that day. The conversation flowed around their jobs for a while, as their drinks sank low in the glasses.

'Do you think Mr George will take you on as a partner? It's great you work for him, but it's a shame it's not full time. I know you still work odd jobs to make up your money'. Jim took another swig of beer, knowing, or thinking he knew, from past discussions the way the conversation would go, a subject they seemed to dance around both face to face and in letters.

'I honestly don't know. There is not enough work for two, but too much work for one. And the farmers vary so much, some appreciate his knowledge and experience, others would rather let an animal die than bring a vet in, any vet! And of course the landowners closer to the town and the city go to the gents who work there'. He looked up at Bea. 'I enjoy the work, that's the thing. I am good at it, or could be in time. I will just have to wait, and do what other work I can'. He waited. Her hand closed tighter around his.

'You could come to London. There are vets working there, you could go to study at the same time. There is other work around, I know you can turn your hand to anything. And we would see much more of each other'. Jim sat closer, the obvious answer to their problems finally out in the open. He had been looking forward to it in many ways, but dreading it also. He ran his fingers through his hair, giving himself time, wanting to engage his brain before answering. He knew it was a tightrope, and he knew there was no right answer.

'I have thought of it, Bea. Probably every day. It seems the obvious thing to do. I want to be with you. I think I could be with you every day and it would not be enough'. Jim looked away, at the bar and then back at the woman he loved. 'I just don't think I can leave my family. Mum's health's not great, and my grandparents are getting no younger, they can't do much work. They rely on my wages. I would feel I am deserting them. It just would not feel right'. He lapsed into silence, finishing his beer before looking back up at Bea. To his surprise she was smiling. 'That's obviously cheered you up, the answer you wanted?!' he said mockingly with a grin, and received a laugh in response.

'I think it's the reply I expected. You're a good man. But please don't say 'No' outright. Just keep the option open. You can't do it now, I understand, but maybe things will change in the future. Don't ever say no'.

'I promise. I love you too much to ever say no', he whispered, and got up to go to the bar, to hide the range of emotions he knew must be showing on his face.

Leaning on the bar, the hubbub in the other room suddenly grew, and individual voices were raised and heard above the general din, one of which sounded an awful lot like Fred Turner.

'I had better go and see what he's got up to now, Bea, back in a moment', he left the snug and went through the door adjoining the two rooms, into the bar, unaware that she immediately got up to follow him, noticing that the noise was increasing with every passing second.

Jim paused as he entered the room, the sight and cause of the consternation obvious immediately. The change in atmosphere cloaked itself around him as he entered, and his eyes scanned the scene in front of him. The bar had maybe nine or ten people in it, a few scattered round the rim of the small room and the benches that encircled it, and the bar to the left with the landlord watching warily and visibly readying himself to join the throng of people in the middle of the floor. Eyes becoming accustomed to the darker, smokier room, Jim saw his granddad Fred facing him about ten feet way, who had his hands on the shoulders of the figure in front. The next man facing him was his old friend Peter's father, Bill, the concern on Fred's face in direct contrast to the rigid anger shown on the younger man's. The third man was in uniform and had his back to Jim, but even without the ability to see his face, he knew that Tom Smith had come back. He sensed rather than saw Bea enter the room behind him, and briefly felt her hand brush off his shoulder as he walked towards the confrontation. Quickly he put himself between Tom and Bill, putting his hands on the Bill's shoulders, aware that whatever had been brewing in the recent minutes was about to explode into the small confined area.

'Leave it Bill, let it go, please'… he could see the colour had drained from the other man's face, not only from the recent events but to Jim's mind a process that had been going on for the last four years. He turned to face Tom, now taller than the bully of his youth, and stronger from his work. 'Why now? There's nothing here for you. Why?'

'I've as much right as any man. Me folks still live here, can't I even visit them? Mum's not got long, stop a man seeing his dying family?'

'Visit them, but you don't come in here' retorted Fred. 'You're not wanted. Just go'. Having turned his head to face Tom, Jim still had both hands on Bill's shoulders, and could feel them sag as whatever energy had driven him to face down the man he thought had caused his son's death began to seep out of his body. The room was silent.

'Come on Bill, he's not worth it', he heard Fred say, as the limp figure was led back to his chair. Jim turned to face Tom. The anger of the events of the last few years, even going back to the orchard as a small child with Bea and the man in front of him, started to fill him from the pit of his stomach and spread through his body, and he could feel himself struggling to control a rage he had always managed to keep under lock and key, until now.

He stepped one pace forward towards the uniformed man, and opened his mouth to speak, when he saw Bea stood behind

Tom to one side of the door, slowly shake her head, her eyes bright and close to tears. He slowly breathed out, making himself relax, keeping his eyes on the woman he adored. He turned back to face the figure in uniform, slowly lent towards his face, and whispered, barely loud enough to hear.

'I'm not a child you can bully now. I know what you tried to do to Bea all those years ago. You broke my arm. See your parents. Don't come back'.

Tom stood for a moment, and Jim could see him considering the options, never taking his eyes off him. Then a smirk appeared, he took a step back, the cocky persona back in place.

'If I must…never liked the beer in here anyway', and turned and strutted out of the room, throwing a brief glance at Bea as he left.

The mood lifted almost immediately. Jim felt a hand clap him on the back, and his Granddad's voice say 'Good lad', but he only had eyes for Bea, still in the same position she had been since they entered the room. The spell suddenly lifted, as she walked towards him and hugged him. He could have stayed like that forever, were it not for the subtle coughs and comments of 'go home if you want do that'. He let Bea go and they smiled.

'This place is far too exciting for me, it never used to be like this! Can you walk me home, Jim? I am staying with my folks tonight, we can have a cup of tea without being centre of attention'.

He smiled back, and turned to speak to his granddad, but Fred and Bill were already engrossed in their game of cribbage, so a swift wave to show he was off, and they turned for the door.

Jim waited in the small entrance-way as Bea went back into the snug to collect her hat, the tension of the situation just a few minutes earlier now entirely free of his body. Her smiling face re-appeared, and he opened the door to let her through and followed close behind. The door slammed behind, and he felt the cool night air and slight breeze on his face, after the close, warm atmosphere he had just enjoyed. No lights outside, just the stars in the clear night sky to see by, but he knew Bea's old family home was only a hundred yards away, and knew the route in his sleep.

Stepping out towards her, he opened his mouth to speak when he was violently pulled back towards the pub by an unknown force behind him, his feet losing their grip on the ground as his back slammed against the pub wall, not hard enough to wind him but powerfully enough to shock him.

His mind was a whirl, the speed with which it had happened and the surprise of it numbing his thoughts. He could see Bea now six feet away in the corner of his eye, and then a punch to the stomach doubled him up and winded him, his legs bending at the knees as his head dropped to the floor. But it wasn't over, what he assumed to be a fist next hitting the side of his head by his temple, as his body crumpled to the side and hit the floor. His face close up to the grass, feeling sick from the attack on his stomach and unable to get this breath, he now felt a trickle of blood down his cheek. Nausea swept through his body, as he opened his mouth wider, desperate to get air into his lungs, and tried to get onto his hands and knees. The taste of blood now in his mouth, he could just distinguish two sets of footsteps, the sound of someone running away at some speed to his right, and to his left coming towards him.

'Oh god, don't get up, take it easy. You're winded, take your time'.

Concern in Bea's voice. On his hands and knees now, Jim just tried to calm himself, concentrating on his breathing and getting something into his lungs. He closed his eyes, the salty taste of blood now reaching his mouth from the cut on his head, and slowly the nausea retreated, and finally he could breathe in and out.

He stayed there for a few, long, seconds, and when the only pain left was from the two punches, he slowly got to his hands and knees, and then stood up. Bea helped him, but Jim knew he was not as bad as feared. The surprise of the attack, and the speed had shocked him and left him unable to defend himself. But now, stood up straight, he started to already feel better. His head seemed to spin for a second, then he put his hand up to his temple, a cut from a ring that must have been on Tom's hand doing the damage. For Tom it most assuredly was. A small bump was rising, and he still had a slightly sick feeling in his stomach. But the damage could have been worse.

'Take your time'.

Bea again, but he could tell from her voice the fear had now dissipated into a general concern. He looked up and could see her better now she was close. Inspecting the side of his face, she confirmed his thoughts.

'A small cut, and you will have a lump, but no bad damage'. She looked directly at him. 'The coward's gone. Let's get you cleaned up, are you alright to walk?'

He nodded, and they slowly moved away, going slowly, but speeding up as the aches eased. The walk to the left and into the village was short, and then left again towards Bea's family home at the end of the lane, holding hands.

Minutes later Jim was sat at the kitchen table, Bea cleaning the side of his face with a wet cloth. The kettle whistled, and she finished drying his skin, put a small plaster on the cut, then moved away to make a pot of tea. Jim watched her. From the moment it had all happened she had been in control, and he was happy to leave it like that.

'I will just see if Mum and Dad want a cuppa, back in a second', she said, touching his arm as she left the room.

Jim stretched, his neck ached slightly, but he felt good. A tea with plenty of sugar would see him right. He mulled over what happened, but it did not take long. It was obvious who it was and what had happened, he was more annoyed with himself that he had not expected it. He swore under his breath, just as Bea returned.

'No need for that, it is not your fault, and I was not expecting it either, so don't do your usual thing and start beating yourself up about it' she ordered, and then crossed over to the sink. Jim smiled at her seeming ability to read his mind. 'Mum and dad are in bed, so we can take these through to the front room. I can get the fire going again, it's still got some embers'. She walked over and gave him his tea, along with a smile and a chaste kiss on his un-bloodied right cheek. 'Extra sugar, you can carry your own cup, beginning to think you're playing on this now', and turned to lead the way into the next room.

The room they entered was dark and cosy, just a couple of candles had been lit, and the fire sparked into life as Bea put a small log onto it, the small flames licking round the curve of wood and growing as the fresh wood fueled them. Bea sat on the thick rug in front of the hearth, and motioned Jim over, so he sat opposite her and laid his cup to the side.

'It's a bit warmer here, let's get the tea into you and make sure you are better before you go'.

'I'm fine' he retorted, 'it was a shock, but all's back to normal now'. He did not want to show any weakness in front of her, and already he was questioning if he could have done anything differently, or better outside the pub.

In the pale light of the room, the evening already started to take on an ethereal glow, as if it had happened a long time ago, or not at all. He took a sip of the still hot tea, and then looked into the flames of the re-awakened fire. The work of the long day, the beer earlier and the excitement in the pub began to takes its toll, and he could feel his eyelids start to feel heavy. The only sound was the crackle of the flames.

'Don't you go to sleep on me, Jim Turner!' Bea's soft voice cut into his reverie, and he looked at her and smiled.

'Sorry, day catching up with me I guess'. Her dark eyes seemed to get darker as she looked back at him, and her pale skin seemed to glow in the reflection of the fire. She smiled, and he realized how so in love he was with her.

'Keep awake, or you'll be falling in the fire', the words meant to be normal, but he thought he could detect a huskiness to the sounds, as though they were driven by more emotion than the words themselves suggested.

She moved from sitting cross legged up onto her knees, and looked at the side of his face that had been cut. Moving across the short distance between them, she knelt inches in front of him, one hand on the floor and the other on his thigh, and inspected the area.

'No lasting damage, just a bump for a couple of days and maybe a scar'. The words hung in the air. Her face was a bare inch from his, and he looked down at the curve of her breasts underneath her blouse, and then up to her open neck and collar bone appearing just where her top opened up after the first button. His throat seemed to constrict, and his stomach tightened as he leant forward and gently kissed her cheek, putting his hand on her waist and then moving down to gently kiss and lick her neck and collar bone. He felt Bea breathe in and her body seemed to tighten, then immediately relax, as she moved her head around and kissed him on his lips, her tongue gently moving inside his mouth as his lips parted.

Moments later she stopped and pulled back, both hands on either side of Jim's face as she looked at him. 'I love you, Jim Turner'. Then she had pushed him back on the rug, their lips together again, Bea working at the buttons on his shirt as he lifted his hand up inside her blouse and caressed her breasts. The years of love, a deep love constrained by the friendship that both had tried to convince themselves was enough for them, enveloped them as they let the deep passion take over.

Quickly Bea moved off Jim and lay by his side, a gap between them created as they both lay, almost in a state of undress, and silently looked at each other, sweat not glistening on their faces.

'I'm a bit scared, Jim.' Bea's eyes looked around, then back at her love. 'I've never done this before. I'm scared.' Jim leant forward and gently kissed her forehead.

'Neither have I, Bea. I don't know what to do. I don't want to hurt you.' He held her hand, bringing it to his lips, and gently kissed it, his eyes closed. They lay silently for a moment. Bea leant forward and whispered in his ear.

'Let's go slow, and work it out together'.

Chapter 14

Jim woke early the next morning, as always the light from the morning sun edging through the curtains at the window and settling across the floor and bed. His eyelids slowly crept open, and almost immediately the slight throb on the left side of his head brought the evening's events back into clarity. Putting his left hand gently towards his head, he felt the bump that had appeared, covered slightly by the cut. He was glad it was no worse, a cold wash and he knew he would be alright, the bump and bruise most likely disappearing within a few days. He gingerly sat up, looking across at the other side of the room. They had split the room as Jim got older, an old pair of curtains, given to them by the neighbours, had been hung from alongside the window across the width of the room, allowing both Jim and his mother a modicum of peace and privacy.

There was no sound from the other side of the curtain, so he swung his legs out of bed and grabbed his clothes, taking them to the bathroom. A cursory look in the mirror confirmed his initial thoughts around the severity of the damage the punch did to his face. Turning the tap on, the ice cold water filled his cupped hands, and as he splashed his face he felt himself slowly waking up more thoroughly, bringing his memories of the rest of the night bobbing to the surface.

They had made love, gently at first, and slowly with more passion. He had stayed what he guessed to be a couple of hours, and the memory of it primarily was being lay in her arms, just content and comfortable in the silence, with just Bea's closeness to him being enough. He would have happily lain there awake all night as she dozed, and as such there was little talk until he came to leave, the fire slowly burning itself out. They quickly dressed, her concern that her parents did not find them alone like that understandable, as much as she was well aware that they knew and liked Jim.

He slowly walked down the stairs, intent on quickly eating some breakfast before heading back over to her house. He knew she was going back to London today, and he wanted to spend every second that he could with her. Opening the kitchen door, he stopped in his tracks, seeing his mother was sat at the table, pot of tea in front of her, and a cup still steaming, her hands wrapped round it as if for warmth. Her face turned to look up at him, and for the second time in the last twelve hours he felt sure he had seen the moment a mask appeared, the drawn lines and tired eyes replaced in a moment, as his mother smiled, straightened her back and looked up at her son. He paused briefly, and chose not to notice this brief moment of delicacy and brittleness in his mother, that she was trying to hide or cover up.

'You were late last night, Jim'. She pulled herself to her feet, and crossed to the cupboard to get a cup as he stood in the doorway, bringing it back to the table and then filling it with the hot tea from the pot. 'How is Bea, I have not seen her for ages?'

Jim blushed as he sat down, but as she passed the cup to him, she placed her other hand on his head.

'Don't worry, even I was young once… not that I can remember it these days! She is a lovely girl. Just be careful. You're both very young'. She kissed his head, and went to cut a slice of bread for him, bringing it over before sitting down again, hands replaced around the cup.

'Thanks Mum. She is … we are just right. It just seems, natural, I guess. Normal'. He looked down at his cup, and started to eat his bread while it cooled. They sat in silence for a moment, Jim wanting to say more, but concern for his mother holding him back every time he thought about speaking. He did not want to talk about Bea's suggestion about London, not with his mother sat in front of him, plainly unwell, and unwilling herself to discuss her own problems.

'I'm surprised you don't follow her, when you both obviously get on so well?' She turned to look at him as she spoke, the smile re-appearing. Jim stared into his cup, wondering if women like Bea and his mother had a sixth sense about these things, they always seemed to know what he was thinking… or was he just that obvious, he face betraying his thoughts without him being aware. 'Has she mentioned it?'

'She has, but I don't know. I want to be with her, but I can't see me in London. My place is here. I enjoy my work, and granddad and gran are here, the church, my other friends. And you'. He had left his mother until last, pretending it was an afterthought so she did not worry, when really she was arguably the main reason.

'Well, you have to do what you feel is right. You are young, you can turn your hand to anything, you're a hard worker, and you're clever… when you can be bothered to show it'. She took a sip of tea, putting the cup down and turned to her son. 'Don't use your family as an excuse. We love you and there will always be a place here for you. If you want to go, then go. But there is no rush to decide, like I said you're still young'. She finished her tea, and got up to move towards the door, putting her hand on his shoulder as she passed. 'Talk to Bea. Right, I need to get dressed, and I suggest you leave before your granddad comes down and interrogates you about last night. I heard all about it when he came in'.

She left Jim alone with his thoughts in the room. She had given him her blessing to leave, taken any pre-conceived ideas about his family responsibility and discarded them. He knew this was about his father. He was aware that she did not want him to take up the slack when his father had left the family all those years ago, not wanting him to be beholden to her or anyone else… he had his own life to lead. Those feelings did not change however, regardless of what she said. The image of her face as she walked in, tired, and was there also pain there? Working multiple jobs to feed and clothe them all, and his grandparents, unable to find work, living off what they could sell and the money his granddad had saved during his working life. How could he leave?

The village was quiet, just starting to stir into life as he strode down the road, back the way he had come a few hours earlier. Chastising himself for it, after the conversation with his mother, he could not help but feel different, a grin emerging as he walked towards Bea, the memories of the previous night still clear and fresh in his mind. He looked up as the house came into view, just as Bea came out of the door and started walking towards him. She looked up, and the joy he felt he could see reflected in her face.

'Well, good morning, fancy seeing you here, meeting anyone in particular?'... He laughed in response as they hugged, and then turned hand in hand to walk back to the Manor House.

'How are you? I was worried I left a bit abruptly, I really wanted to stay'.

'I am good, I promise. It's alright, you had to go, and the thought of my parents coming in was not great! How is the cheek, it looks swollen, but nothing too severe?'

'It's fine, done far worse over the years! Shall certainly have clear memories of last night for a long time'.

Bea smiled, and they walked on, soon coming to the drive, and Jim felt the sick feeling in his stomach of not seeing her for months growing with every step. Eyes down as the thoughts of months apart seemed to slow his steps and weigh him down, he saw some freshly flowering white roses in the borders around the front of the house, and on a whim let go of Bea's hand, and rushed over, quickly snapping the flower and top two inches of the stalk off in is hand, as he heard 'Jim!' behind him.

‘It’s for you, on your trip back to London’ he explained, putting it into the buttonhole of her jacket. ‘I want you to see it and remember last night’. Pulling the rose down by the stalk, he caught his finger on the thorn and muttered under his breath, to an accompanying giggle.

‘Are you ever going to be romantic with me and not injure yourself in some way at the same time?’

‘It’s obviously the affect a beautiful woman has on me’. Jim leant forward and kissed her on the lips as she wrapped her arms around his neck.

‘Thank you, Jim Turner! Now, I have work to do. Don’t forget to write!’

‘I will. I love you, Bea. So much’. She chastely kissed him on the cheek.

‘I know, so we are just lucky that I love you too, I guess. See you in the summer… and think about what we discussed! For me.’ And she was gone, rushing into the house, leaving him alone on the drive.

Chapter 15

Bea was lucky enough to travel to the train station at the next town in the car. Mr Carmichael, who she worked for by tutoring his children, had recently purchased a car to be kept at the Manor House, one of a few that seemed to be springing up in the local area. They had gone back to London the day before as a family, and she was left to her thoughts on the train down. Looking out of the window at the trees, farms and fields that rushed by, Bea pondered about her request to Jim. From early in her life, she had known that she would need to take action for herself to get anywhere in life. The village and surrounding areas did not offer opportunity or work for women, any more or less than the country as a whole. Despite the slow changes that seemed to be brewing in the capitol, driven by the suffragette movement, and some of the more liberal politicians in power. And her parents had limited means, having just one daughter, her father working in the factory in the town, and her mother keeping the home. So it was down to her.

Schoolwork was done well, and on time, and to the best of her ability, even the subjects she had less interest in. And any moment free at school, she offered to help the master in charge, so that when the time came to leave, the old man had needed her to stay. The work she had done had lessoned his load to the point that when she stood in front of him to say goodbye for the final time, the realization that he would struggle without her help descended on him like a black cloud. Within hours the subject had been broached with the local church, and Bea had found herself back at school the following term, helping as she had done before, and taking on some cleaning work around the school.

Like Jim, she had also worked and earned where else she could, in the fields fruit picking in the summer, and helping out at the Manor House when large events were being held. They always took on a few extra hands from the village during this time, and again, Bea took her opportunity, working well and rising above the other part timers taken on, so when the opportunity of a position arose, her name was the first that came up in conversation. And when the first of three children arrived, and the Carmichaels heard that Bea was already teaching at the school, the next step on the ladder was taken, as she found herself teaching the village children in the mornings, and the Carmichaels in the afternoons.

Bea sighed as she looked forward out of the window, and the outskirts of the metropolis appeared in the distance, the greens and golds of the fields giving way to the grey and black of the housing and city buildings appearing over the horizon where the track was heading. And therein lay the problem in Bea's mind. As a teacher cum nanny, her time, she saw, was coming to an end. The eldest child had gone to boarding school at Christmas, and the next was due to go after the summer holidays. The youngest would be leaving in twelve to eighteen months, and where would that leave her? Either taken on as a maid, or let go, with a choice of going back to the village, or finding a job elsewhere in London.

The train left the stretch of fields, and the walls of houses and tenements rose either side of the train, scenery into the distance reduced from miles to feet in a few seconds. She wanted Jim to come down, and wanted them together, but what was her future right now? She knew he would succeed and thrive wherever he was, but was aware of the ties that bound him to his family and home. She knew he wanted to be with her, as much as she wanted him there. Could she push him to do that, drive him into a future of uncertainty, when her own solid world of the last five years was itself starting to pull apart at the seams?

Pulling into Waterloo station, Bea collected her two bags and stepped off the platform. The station was busy, trains filling each platform as city society went to and fro' on its way across the station, businessmen mixing with families, and she also saw some soldiers dotted around. Striding towards the exit, she caught sight of one of the footmen from the house, and within minutes they were sat in a cab heading away from the hustle and bustle of the station to the four story house on the outskirts of the city that was now home to her.

'Glad you're back?'

Bea looked up to see Elsie, the maid, appear in the doorway, and got up from the packing to hug her friend, who she shared the room with in the eaves of the house.

'Yes, and no, I guess. I missed the children, and you obviously, but it was lovely to see Jim.' A sad smile, and she turned away quickly, as she felt the tears close to the surface. She would not do that, certainly not in front of anyone.

'Oh yes, tell me more! How is Jim? You two getting to know each other, err, better?' Bea could hear the suggested question in her friend's voice, surreptitiously wiping away a stray tear that may have made it onto her face and turned back to look at Elsie.

'Well, wouldn't you like to know? Maybe we know each other better, maybe we don't. That's for you to find out!' The maid moaned, and slumped on the bed.

'Bah, you're no fun! Give a girl a morsel of gossip at least! There's been nothing going on here while you have been away'.

'Hmm, I doubt that.' Bea finished putting her few things away. 'You have the afternoon off? Let's go somewhere, just for a walk. I've been stuck on that train, I need to stretch my legs'.

'Definitely, let me change and lets go…I can drag some more details out of you!'

The road the house lay on was busy with pedestrians and traffic, so they turned north and headed towards the local park, an oasis of green in the grey desert of bricks and mortar. City life rushed around them and they made their way down the road, blessed with a few hours to themselves before they would both have to return to their working lives. The road ended in a junction, and as they crossed during brief slowing of the rush of traffic, the grass, trees, and pathways of the park opened up in front of them. Even on a weekday afternoon, the park was busy. Mostly mothers pushing children in prams, or with older children playing around them. They slowly walked toward the lake in the middle, where they knew there would be a stall selling drinks. Elsie quickly grabbed one of the few remaining benches in the sea of families orbiting around the lake, and Bea brought two glasses of lemonade over.

'It's warm, but it's wet, better than nothing'.

It was a warm spring day, and the talk went over the events of the last few days in the house, while Bea filled Elsie in on her time back home. She looked around the park and the lake in front of them, and found herself looking at the few courting couples who were out. That had been her and Jim for a couple of evenings in the last week, but already it seemed so far away. The events of last night could have happened months ago, rather than under a day.

'Penny for them? You were away with the fairies, Bea'.

'Am I that obvious? Just thinking about the last week. I really did have a wonderful time, but it all passes by so quickly. You look forward to it for so long, and it passes in an instant'. Thoughts of the night before passed through her mind as she spoke, the warm feeling of time spent at home slowly dissipating as truth of her situation crowded out the happy memories. 'We want to be together, I just don't see how'. The statement hung in the air as Bea stared into the distance, eyes drawn again to the couples navigating the park in front of her.

'You have to talk, love. You can't decide alone, it's something you both have to agree on and work towards'. Elsie emptied her glass, quenching her thirst, mulling the situation over. 'It's here or there, the way I see it. You go to him, or he comes to you. If you are together, where will you have the most support, and chances of work?'

'That's the problem. Here, we have everything the city offers. At home, we would have our family's support'. Bea did not like to say that it could almost be them supporting the family, it would be unfair. How much of Jim's reticence was genuine? Or was it an excuse to hang his hat on, the thought of moving one he just could not consider, even for her.

'Well, I'm a city girl, so don't know about your village life, or your family'. She looked at Bea and held her hand. 'But I do know you have to talk and make a decision. Next time you go, yes?' Bea glanced back.

'Yes, next time', knowing in her mind it always seemed to be next time, as she never pushed the subject hard enough, and Jim avoided it, loathe to make a decision that he thought would never satisfy them both or everyone.

'Do what's right for you two' finished Elsie, standing up, seeming to read her friend's mind 'Family are family, work is work, you need to put yourself first'.

Bea got up, held Elsie's hand, and they walked back around the lake, heading back towards the house. None the wiser as to the outcome, after the conversation, she did think Elsie's last point was the most pertinent. Speak to Jim, and do what they thought was best for them. The problem was getting Jim to agree to that.

Chapter 16

The Reverend Steed stood at the church doorway, as the parishioners queued to leave the church, desire to get out into the open air and away dampened somewhat by the understanding that the cool of the building was in stark contrast to the heat of the day outside. June had been pleasant, but July had seen the temperature rise day by day. By winter the older folk were often heard to complain about the cold, and those same people were now walking round the village, voicing their opinion on the heat to all who would listen, as well as those who did not wish to. Previous summers were offered as comparisons, both as support for their argument and against. Each said a few words to the vicar, some brief and to the point, while others the reverend had to subtly move on, knowing they would be talking until evensong if he let them.

Jim dawdled at the back of the queue, watching the crowd of people slowly dwindle bit by bit, until it was just himself, slowly moving towards the reverend. The verger nodded an acknowledgement before stepping away and back towards the pulpit. Jim watched him go, and a voice pulled his attention back.

'Hello Jim, nice to see you this morning. Did you enjoy the sermon?'

'Yes, Vicar, very much so. How are you?'

'Oh, well as can be expected for a man of my advanced years!' He raised an eyebrow, as if challenging Jim to deny it, but only received a smile in response. 'Now then lad, I saw you hanging around by the font just now, it fair took me back all those years to when you snuck in here one Sunday! Old habits, eh? I am guessing you want a chat? Let me change and I will meet you in the lane in five minutes. I am walking into the village, a bit of company in this heat would not go amiss'. He smiled at Jim and was gone, leaving him to belatedly follow where the others had tread, out of the aged building and into the bright sunshine beyond.

The lane was empty, the sun beat down on the road, and Jim found some shade a few yards from the entrance to the church, sitting on a bench under a solitary yew tree. The world was silent, the only thing seemingly alive being a single bee, moving from flower to flower amongst the wild flowers that ran alongside the church. He leant back and closed his eyes, enjoying the peace and quiet after the usual six and a half days of hard work from morning to night. In the peace he heard the sound of the church door being shut and locked, and opened his eyes to see Reverend Steed walking towards him across the grass.

'I thought you may had been asleep, my apologies for taking some time. There is always some trifle or other the verger needs me to sort out before I leave. Shall we?' Jim got up and followed the older man to the lane, and down towards the road that led to the village. 'I hope you don't mind us going this way, but lovely as the path through the orchard is, I prefer to have it firm underfoot at my age, and also like to avoid anything that needs climbing over'. They reached the end of the lane and turned towards the village, Jim thinking that having mentioned his age twice, maybe the vicar had as many insecurities about his age as anyone else, being a man of the cloth was still no protection against the advancing years.

They slowly strolled down the hill in silence, the older man wanting to leave Jim to decide when to bring up whatever it was he wanted to discuss. It helped not to push, experience had taught him, and was generally an easier and more open conversation if the other person started when they were ready. He looked sideways at Jim, and as he did so the youngster started to talk, almost taking him by surprise.

'Did you always want to be in the church? Was it what you wanted to do, or was there another job…. Did you have a choice?'

It was not the line of questioning that Steed had expected, but from knowing Jim all his life, and being aware of what had been happening in it, he could see where the conversation was going to head. As was usual for this young lad, as honest and straightforward as he generally was, the option of taking a different tack was never far away with him.

'Well, it was always likely, Jim. My father had a parish in Dorset, and I grew up in and around the church. From a young age I wanted to follow in my father's footsteps… wanted to be him. In those days the church really was the centre of village life. I think, as a boy… remember, I too was once a child! As a boy, I saw the way he could help people, and support them. That's what drew me, being there for others'.

'You never wanted to do anything else? You never made a choice?'

'Well, in some ways. I was lucky enough to go to Oxford, and I spent some of my youth in Europe, as was the fashion at that time. But I was always going to come back to the church'. Reverend Steed looked at Jim, and thought a hastening of the conversation would help the boy. 'I can't tell you what to do, Jim, and I fear that's maybe what brought you to me. I was always going to serve the Lord, despite a few wrong turns and diversions along the way. But it is something I wanted to do in my heart, and these was no-one around to take my heart another way'.

They both stood to one side, as two young children ran up the path and past them, oblivious to the world around them. Reverend Steed's eyes followed them, before looking back at the torn youth in front of him.

'I can't tell you what to do, I have never been in your position. What I can tell you, because I know it to be true, is that those who love you won't berate you, or cast you aside in some way whatever decision you make. And decisions can be changed. The village will always be here'.

He put his arm on Jim's shoulder and they moved off, the village now close where their ways would part. Jim was thinking about the older man's words, working out if they made his decision any easier, when the curate's voice cut into his thoughts one last time.

'The one thing I can advise you to do is enjoy your life as much as you can. I fear there is an ill wind brewing on the continent. Man always seems to revert to violence, usually as a first or second resort rather than the final one'. His words came out almost as a sigh, and as Jim scanned his face he seemed to have aged in the short walk down the hill form the church. 'Make your decision, lad, and put every fibre of your being into making it work. And if it does not, come back to us here'. They had reached the centre of the village, and the Reverend touched his hat and left Jim to walk up to his grandparent's house.

Chapter 17

The English lesson had not been going well. Jack, the middle child of three, was having one of those days, where complete concentration was always just out of his grasp. One minute he was all intense focus, the next he was looking out of the window into the street beyond, the world going by outside was of far greater interest to a young boy stuck in a room with his teacher. Bea had given him the benefit of the doubt until now, but her patience and own interest was starting to wear thin. The last days of July had started to bring some warmer weather, and that had continued into early August, and for one of the few times in her life, teaching in the study was the last place she wanted to be.

The last few days, after seemingly months of growing anticipation in the city, had brought simmering events slowly to the boil. The Government had been in daily, if not hourly, discussion and negotiation with Germany, for the preceding month or so, ever since the Archduke's assassination. Bea followed it as much as she could, and had the benefit of hearing direct from Mr Carmichael, who appeared to be in close contact with at least two members of parliament in his Club. No one really wanted war, or at least none of the friends Bea had, and she was unsure of her own beliefs. War itself was as a pointless exercise, mainly driven by greed and the expansion of various empires, British, Ottoman and Prussian. And the reason for going to war seemed to rest almost entirely on who controlled which trade routes, though she chastised herself for holding his maybe simplistic viewpoint. However, she thought potentially the war would give her more opportunity than she had known in her life. London was alive, you could feel it walking the streets, as if some great change were about to happen. And Bea intended to make the most of it. Not just for her but for Jim too.

'Have we finished, Miss Beatrice?' Jacks question brought her back into the room from her thoughts, and a good thing too. She could hardly chastise the boy for not focusing on school work when she could barely control her own attention span. The clock struck one, and from the corner of her eye she saw Mr Carmichael climb the steps to the house. He rarely came home at this hour, and Bea felt excitement, or fear, she was not sure which, begin to make itself known in the pit of her stomach.

'Well Jack, I think we have done enough for the day. Just this once, you can pack your things away'. A barely suppressed 'yes' escaped the boys mouth, as he packed his school things away in the study.

'Miss Beatrice, could you join us in the parlour with Jack?' Mr Carmichael's face appeared round the door then went again, barely having finished his sentence. Turning to tell Jack, she was already too late, the boy rushing past her to the door, something in his young mind telling him something was up. His father never came in the study during schooling, and he rushed out of the door, the child's excitement a counterpoint to Bea's own slight unease.

When she arrived in the next room, she noticed Mrs Carmichael and their daughter Jean were already there. The head of the house did not delay his announcement, his face stern and Bea noticed that he never took his eyes off his wife, holding their youngest child. The room was silent in expectation.

'I've been at the club, and have it on good authority that we are likely to be at war with Germany before the day is out. Asquith has sent an ultimatum that the Germans are unlikely to accede to.' The words were uttered through pursed lips. No one spoke, just a slight gasp from Bea's mistress, as Carmichael addressed his wife. 'I suggest we go to the Manor House today and you and the children spend the summer there. I will return tomorrow to see what needs to be done here. Miss Beatrice, you will be kind enough to accompany us. I feel the children will be safer there. The train leaves at two, pack what you need, and I will arrange for anything else to be sent up when I come back tomorrow'. He paused, went to say something more, a but then changed his mind, kissed his wife, and left the room in silence.

'Come on, let's get you ready, nothing will happen stood here'. Bea spoke to get herself moving as much as anything, and chivvied Jack out of the room, slowly followed by the others.

The next hour was spent packing her own things, little as there was, before Bea went and helped get the children's things together with Elsie.

'You take care, Bea. And if you get chance to stay there with your man, do it! Don't come back here, the city is not the place to be during a war. Look after yourself, my girl.'

'Oh Elsie, I will be fine, and so will you. It can't last that long, before long we will be back to normal.'

'You say it, but your eyes are saying something else, I think.'

They quickly hugged, with no time for goodbyes, and within minutes they were in a taxi-cab heading for Waterloo station.

Everything seemed the same to Bea as the last time she had arrived a few months before. People just carried on with their business, the platforms the usual hubbub of city life going to and fro. Bea questioned what they were doing, was war really inevitable? Nothing had changed, was it an over-reaction? Then walking along the platform, she heard the newspaper boy and saw the headline, as though he had been there to remove any doubts… 'War Inevitable!'…'Ultimatum Sent To Kaiser'… and small group of people moving towards the seller, paying and walking away, some slowly, some at speed, as the message hit home.

'Quickly Bea!'

For the second time in a few hours Jack had dragged her back to reality, and she turned and moved towards the open door of the train, the guard helping the family into first class. Bea got on last, catching a final look down the platform to the throng of people beyond, and wondered if or when she would be here again. A whistle sounded, the guard walking along the platform with his flag held in the air, as she slammed the door and the city was slowly left behind.

Sitting in her seat with the family in first class, Bea's memory again went back to her last journey on the train, back in the early spring but travelling in the other direction. Her mind was full then of her life with Jim, and the permutations around them both. Nothing seemed an obvious answer at the time, the defining factor being Jim and the course that he wanted to take. How would this turn of events change that, if at all? The fields, towns and villages rushed by as the train sped north, and her time was spent keeping Jack amused and entertained in the carriage.

'I'm sure I will feel better back at the Manor House. City life may suit my husband, but I feel more at home back in the country'.

Mrs Carmichael smiled at Bea as she said it. She had known Bea since she had been a little girl, helping out at the house, and always spoke to her openly, as she did with all of the staff. It was the reason, or one of the reasons, all of the staff were so loyal to the family. The intimation of friendship rather than ownership, even if they truth were less palatable. At least, they were good employers.

'Yes', she replied,' It will be good to be back'.

Jack had dropped off to sleep, a mixture of boredom and tiredness taking over his body, and Jean had been asleep in the Nanny's arms since they left Waterloo.

‘Will you be needing me this evening, do you think? I would like to see my parents if I can, they were not expecting me, and they will worry if the news of the war has reached them’.

‘Of course, you must see your parents. And the Turner family, of course’.

Mrs Carmichael smiled as she offered this last comment. In knowing Bea so long, she had an idea of the girl’s friendship with the young veterinarian. And as such, wondered, as Bea did, how long before things changed, driven by the war, or just time moving on.

‘Yes, I will see Jim if he is free’.

‘How are you two, if I may be so bold as to ask? Do you have any plans for the future? We don’t often get chance to talk’.

‘Not yet. Jim is working hard, and I spend my time in London, so we don’t really plan. We just do what we can’.

‘Of course, you do a wonderful job, the children adore you. But, they are getting older. Jack will be going to boarding school soon’. She stroked her sons head, and then turned to check her youngest. ‘I will keep you with us for as long as we need you’. She paused, choosing her words carefully. ‘You do such a fine job. But I think you may want to discuss things with Jim further, while you are here?’ Mrs Carmichael’s head dropped, as she sighed, then looked up and straight at Bea again. ‘I am sorry, I am making a mess of this. It’s because you are such a part of the family, and we have known you so long, it’s so hard. I think we may have to let you go at Christmas. Jack will be moving to boarding school in January, and there just won’t be a position. I’m sorry, Bea. We will give you a fine reference, and I know some friends who are looking for a tutor for their children. If you agree, I will put your name forward. But speak to Jim while you are here. You may want to make your own plans, away from London’.

She stopped speaking and looked out of the window, plainly struggling or embarrassed by what she had said, and the difficulty in saying it. Bea was not sure how she felt, a slight shock maybe, but no more. It was something that she had expected, just not right now, bare hours after finding that the country was at war and being rushed onto a train and away from the capital. She had some time, that was the main thing, and at least she would be able to discuss it with her parents and Jim. She smiled, a decision had to be made, and all this did was to bring it forward.

'Thank you for telling me, Maam. I appreciate your honesty. I will speak to my parents and Jim. Thank you for your kind offer of a reference and an alternate position elsewhere'.

Mrs Carmichael looked up, eyes brighter and smiled back. She had been putting the conversation off for too long, and with the announcement by her husband earlier in the day, she felt it was only right to let the young girl know, so that she could make her own arrangements for her future life. She also felt a weight had been lifted off her own shoulders.

'I am glad you took it so well. Do give my regards to your parents and Jim when you see them, though I am sure I will see them in church soon'.

Bea nodded, and looked back out of the window. The train was moving towards Oxford, half of the journey gone. The question is, she thought to herself, will my life lead me to come back on this train, to stay in the village, or take me somewhere entirely knew. The desire to be back as soon as possible rose within her, as she felt sure the decision would be made at the end of the journey.

Chapter 18

Jim woke early as usual, the light of the morning sun filling the bedroom. Slowly sitting up, the drowsiness of sleep sliding off him with the sheets, he heard muffled voices downstairs. Turning, the silence the other side of the room told him he was alone. He rose and quickly dressed for another working day, heading downstairs, creases furrowing his brow as he mulled over why everyone would be up at this time.

'All the men will be gone, who are old enough, you mark my words'.

His granddad's voice, the speaker turning to look at his grandson upon entering. Jim saw his saw mother and granddad were sat round the kitchen table, while his gran was stood boiling the kettle on the stove to fill the pot of tea.

'Morning, what are you talking about? What's happened?'

'It's war, lad. Postman told us not ten minutes ago. It's in the papers. Happened last night, the Germans had a chance to back off, but didn't't'.

'What does it mean for us? What's going to happen?'

'Everything will change, and nothing, most likely. It'll be a waiting game, but hopefully they will all come to their senses. Politicians! Going to war when there's barely enough money to feed their own folk!' His Granddad's opinions drove his voice higher, the mixture of fear and anger waging their own war on his mood.

'Well, hopefully it won't affect us' opined Jim's mum, 'they can fight their war and leave us out of it, we have enough problems of our own without concerning ourselves with this'.

'Won't affect us? The lad will be gone, how will it not affect us? We barely have an army these days, they will be recruiting, you mark my words, he will be gone'.

'I am here, Granddad. Won't the choice be mine? If I don't want to go, I won't, surely?'

Fred grunted and looked down at his coffee, cowed by the glare falling on him from his wife and daughter.

'I'm just saying, that's all'. He picked up his tea and left the room, putting his hand on Jim's shoulder as he did. Jim's mum stood up and gave him his tea.

'We don't know what will happen, so let's just wait and see. No point getting het up about something that may or may not happen'. She kissed him on the cheek, and close up Jim thought she looked more tired than ever… no colour in her face, crow's feet more obvious than ever before. 'And the posty also brought some gossip, as well. Seems the war announcement has changed some people's plans higher up than us, and the Carmichaels are back in residence at the Manor House'. She smiled, and turned and left the room, following in the footsteps of her father.

The morning was spent working for Bill George. Work was quieter, and they slowly made their way from farm to farm. The cloudless sky stretched out in front of them as they journeyed from job to job, the heat of the day seeming to rise with each mile passed. Each farmer had heard the news in a variety of ways, and each one had his own opinions regarding what would happen and how they would be affected. 'They will want us to work harder and produce more, but more'n likely take the youngsters away from us at the same time' was a typical opinion, the person voicing it invariably giving Jim a sideways glance before moving back to work. There were also some, Jim noticed, who did not think it would affect them. 'London's war, not ours'. Time would tell who would turn out to be correct.

'You've got a job with me as long as you want it, Jim. Or as long as I need you, don't you worry about that'.

'Thanks Bill'.

The cart was driven away, leaving Jim in the middle of the village in the middle of the day. Looking both ways, home and towards Bea's, and on a whim he headed towards her parent's house. If she had been in touch they would know, and would also know when she was going to be free to see him. The whole world seemed to have changed since he had woken that morning, and he felt the only person he could really talk to about it was Bea.

To his surprise, it was Bea herself who answered the door. Shock turned to joy as they hugged tightly, Jim feeling that he could happily stay like this and never let go. The time apart seemed an age, yet their moments together seemed to fly by. He kissed her gently on the cheek, and took a step back.

'I didn't expect to see you, I thought you would be up at the house?'

'I have the rest of the day off. The children are with their mother for the day'. And getting used to me not being there, she thought, but quickly buried the idea, something to be sorted in the future, but not right now. 'Are you free? It's a lovely day again, let's go for a walk. I was stuck in a train most of yesterday and then in a classroom today, I need to stretch my legs'.

Bea called back into the house to tell her parents she was going out, slammed the door behind her and put her hand into the crook of Jim's arm. They walked to the road, and crossed to the footpath leading to the orchard and church, bringing each other up to date on their lives as they went, along with the subject of the news on the war.

'I guess you always knew the job would finish, with the children off to boarding school? It's a shame it's so soon. What will you do?' They had reached the orchard, where there were still some pickers moving up and down the rows, the fruit starting to thin out now, but still plenty of work for a few weeks. Bea sat down, back against the trunk of a tree, and Jim slumped down beside her in the shade.

'It depends on you. I can stay in London, doing the same work but for someone else. Mrs Carmichael said as much, and I do enjoy the work, and the city'. She lay down, with her head on his lap, and looked up at him. 'It's down to you. I don't want to live apart, but don't want to lose you. We can't go on like this, seeing each other every few months for a couple of weeks. And if I did stay, there would be no reason to come back up here'. It had been said, and just in saying it Bea felt a weight lift. They could not be together at such a distance, no matter how hard they tried.

Jim looked away, out of the orchard and towards the hills in the distance. Not a day had passed by in the last few months when he had not considered this situation. He had made a decision. Maybe the news of the morning had skewed matters, but he could not help that now.

'I will come down to London to be with you. If that's where you want to be, and not here, then I will come down. If I can't get any veterinary work, I will find something else. Maybe just outside London. I want to be with you Bea.' He leant forward brushed her lips with his, then went on. 'But I have to sort this with my family first, and have their agreement, know they will be alright. And Bill George, I have to speak to him'. He stroked her hair, and smiled. 'If you agree, I will come down in the new year, after Christmas. Let me sort things out here, and see what this war brings, if anything. You can stay in your job, hopefully get the new job, then I will come down to you. I love you'.

Bea got to her knees, leant forward, and kissed the man she loved. 'And I love you too, Jim Turner'. She was surprised, feeling his need to support his family would keep him home, but it was a pleasant surprise, as she wrapped her arms around him and they held each other.

The walk back to the village was a slow one. Jim contemplated his decision, unsure even to the last moment what he would say, but content he had done the right thing. Time would tell if he had not, but for the moment it felt right, and that was all that mattered.

Chapter 19

'I know you want to go lad, and I don't blame you. But life's changed. The countries at war, and sooner or later the government will call people into the army'. Fred had been sat in the garden, working on his vegetable patch, and with the women not there his opinions came to the fore. After seeing Bea, they had arranged to meet at the pub in the evening, giving Jim a chance to speak to his family, and at first, seeing his granddad he thought this would be the easier way. Speak to him alone, get him onside. His granddad had always been supportive, putting Jim's side to the fore whenever a disagreement came up, fighting his corner. Subtly trying to replace the father who had walked out. But it had not panned out that way, or at least it did not seem to.

'The war won't affect me granddad. It's for the army, professional soldiers, not people like me. I'm a country boy, who tries to fix animals!'

'If you think that, you will be very much mistaken. They will be wanting men… men to fight, yes, even men there to take care of the animals. It's a fight for the country, lad. All of us… and it's our duty to fight'.

Jim had not seen his granddad so vehement, about any subject. For the first time, ever, they started to lock horns, which was something neither wanted. Jim physically and emotionally stepped back, and stooped down to help with the weeding. Fred got down by him.

'It's your duty, my lad. Bea's not going anywhere, you're both young, and have the rest of your lives'. Kneeling in the soil, his hand came up and rested on Jim's shoulder. 'You want to go, it is the right decision. Don't worry about us, we will cope. And your mother is strong, always was! But just think about it. Bea's got a job, and then it sounds like she could have another? Six months will fly past'. Putting his hand back on the ground, the weeding continued. 'Just think about it, that's all I am saying. Plenty round here will volunteer. So just think'.

Jim felt there was no right answer, feeling bad about leaving his parents and grandparents as it was, his granddad had now thrown another suggestion at him, the thought of joining the army before seeing Bea. More confused than ever, he did not reply, concentrating on the small weeds growing round the cabbages in front of him.

'And the pay will be better than now'. Fred had obviously not finished his speech. 'Six months more money than you are on now… being clothed and fed'. Jim looked up, but his granddad was already getting up. 'It's up to you lad'. He threw the weeds they had both plucked into the wheel barrow, steering it towards the compost heap at the top of the garden. Jim just stared after him, confusion clouding his mind more than ever.

The pub was quiet that evening when Jim arrived, having arranged to meet Bea outside. The conversation with his Granddad had been rolling around his mind all that afternoon and early evening, ever since he had had the option of joining up dropped on him out of the blue. The subject had started to come up when they had eaten earlier, but he had seen a steely look from his gran directed at his granddad that had crushed the subject before its flowering. The meal was then finished in silence, before his Mum met him at the door on the way out.

'Do what you want to do, ignore my father, and anyone else who offers advice. All you do is what's right for you and Bea'.

But what was right? He wanted Bea to come back here, but there would be nothing for her work wise, and he would not make her do that. She had worked hard to get the position she had now, he would not dream of taking that away from her. He looked down the lane to where she would appear, just in time to see her appear round the corner with her father. So London was the only option, where she had the opportunity to work, while he would have to find work. Maybe it was the best solution, even if it meant leaving his family. But now his granddad had unwittingly provided a third way, to join the army, be fed, watered and paid for six months while Bea worked. Then the war would be over by the end of the year, all the newspapers he had seen that evening said so. He could send money to his family, and then join Bea in London in what was six months? They had known each other since they were little, and even now spent months apart because of work, what was a few more months?

He looked up again at the approaching steps getting louder, and smiled as Bea arrived in her father's stead. 'Don't look so worried, lad, I am going in the bar, well away from you youngsters', and was gone after kissing his daughter on the cheek.

The snug was cool after the warmth of the summer day outside, and quiet compared to the noise and hubbub of the bar next door. 'Young lads getting excited about the war', explained the landlord, 'ignorance is bliss, so they say', he went on, in a resigned voice. Jim smiled in response, turning to join Bea.

'Last time I was in here you got yourself into some bother, I remember Mr Turner! I hope that does not happen again… even though the rest of the evening was rather special'. Jim felt his face redden, and took a swig of beer, coughing in the attempt to cover up his embarrassment.

'I promise not to get into any fights! Well, not in here at least'. Subtle it was not, he thought, but he needed to discuss what was on his mind, and sooner rather than later.

'Not in here? You thinking of fighting somewhere else then?' The smile had dropped from her face as she took a sip of drink, but her eyes stayed fixed on him.

'Nothing's changed, I promise. I will move to London, I want to be with you'. He reached out to hold her hand. 'I was thinking I may volunteer for the army. Wait, hear me out!' Bea had opened her mouth to give her opinion and the look on her face reflected her thoughts. 'You have a job until January, and then with luck will have another to move to. Everyone says it won't last long. I can earn more money in the army than I can working for Bill, and picking fruit. I can send it home to my Mum, so they will be OK. Then when it's over I will join you in London'.

Saying it made it sound more real, but at the same time more risky. But Jim thought it made sense, the more he said it. He could do the right thing by Bea, and earn money for his family, who would be worse off when he moved. It seemed like a perfect solution.

'What if the war doesn't end soon?' Bea had been surprised by Jim's suggestion. She could see the benefits, but unlike him she could see the pitfall in his plan. 'What if it goes on for longer? The Boar War went on for years. What if this is the same? What if you can't leave the army?' She let go of his hand. 'Have you thought this through?' The concern on her face was plain to see. Why risk it? If he had to fight, then the decision was made, but why volunteer? Why offer yourself up?'

'It will be for the duration. So, I guess 6 months is what they say, but if it is a year, then it's a year. That's not long, Bea. I will have my life here, I will have my life in the army, and then I can come to London knowing more than I do now. All I know is this countryside, these villages and hamlets. All I can offer London now is my small knowledge of veterinary work and agriculture, what will that do for me in London. I need to see more, to learn more, experience more'. He leant forward and held her hand again. 'The more I know and learn the better I can support us'.

'I can support myself! I have been until now'. Bea's shoulder slumped, the anger gone as soon as it arrived. 'I'm sorry. I know what you mean. I just worry. It's just that everything has changed in few days. Before it was either London or here. Now it's the war and who knows where that will take us?'

Chapter 20

He had joined up the day after his last night with Bea in the village. Again returning to her parent's house after leaving the pub, repeating the early morning rise and return to his grandparents that he had first travelled a few months earlier. However this time, the mood was subdued. They had talked more, and had come to an understanding and agreement about his decision. Bea remained unconvinced, though she hid it well the following morning. This would be their last parting, a few minutes together after he had left his parents that morning, before he left to move on to the next village to sign up.

'You just make sure you come back soon. I will stay in London, and work out my next job. But I won't wait forever! You are not the only man around, Turner!'

They hugged, and chastely kissed, a small group of other young men, mostly boys Jim had been at school with, still managing to thrown comments at them and whistle.

'Behave you lot! Wasn't that long ago I was helping teach you lot at school!' She received a cheer for her efforts, and Jim let go of her hand and moved away.

'I will write when I can, Bea, and will see you first chance I get'. He turned and walked off with the other men, not daring to turn around, and not seeing the misery that seeped down her face the moment he left.

For weeks, training was no more than camping in a field, little uniform to go round, and what there was seemed to be overly large or ridiculously small. For a large time the men were in their own clothes, before some blue army uniforms appeared for a short period, which Jim thought made him look more like a postman than a soldier. He even got some leave to go home, and managed to see his mother and grandparents. Thoughts turned to the war, and what little seemed to be happening. The extra money was good, and was helping at home, but was this what everyone expected? Maybe he should have stayed at home, or just moved to London.

Then everything started to move forward at a rush in October. Within a few weeks, uniforms, weapons and training were all supplied and completed. Rumours spread faster than orders, and Jim learnt that they were due to be sent to France at the end of October. Within days, he found himself on a train going to the coast, packed to the rafters with soldiers, freshly trained and uniformed, knowing nothing of what would await them. No more cheering crowds at the port as they departed, the early days of the war long gone.

Six months had passed, and within the first few weeks any rose tinted images Jim had of the war and seeing the world were swept aside. When he first arrived the race to the coast was in earnest, as both sides dug in to hold their positions, settling in for the long term. There was no semblance of what they had been told war would be like in training… open warfare a thing of the past, as trenches were extended north and south and the enemies faced off across a hundred yards of nothing.

Everything became routine to Jim. Time in the front line, an almost constant state of fear, moved back to the support trenches, then time off in reserve. Then repeat. Hours and days of boredom interspersed with times of sheer terror… going over the top, and under bombardment. Death became routine. Jim thought back to the life he was used to, going on his rounds with Bill George, covering miles of countryside every day, and now his life was contracted to just a few yards of dugout, and the men around him.

He knew he had been lucky in those first few months. The odd scratch and cut, while he saw men he had trained with die around him. Marching along the road, Jim thought back to the letters he had written. He lied. He kept upbeat with his mother, and grandparents. He did not want them to worry. And he was better paid than of old, he had one period of leave when he went home and left some money. But he was almost glad to be back after the day he had back in the village. The lack of change there was disturbing, compared to what he had been through and the life he was living, and he felt less himself than he did sat in a dugout. Not sure what to say, or how to act, it was almost a blessing to them all when he left. His granddad was quiet. So quiet.

Bea kept him going, through the letters they exchanged. The Carmichaels were keeping her on until the end of January, then she had already been accepted for a job as tutor by the new family. He had not heard from her for a couple of weeks, but it was to be expected with the start of a new job and moving there. He wrote every other day. It was the one time he could forget about what was going on around him, and lose himself in the life he had led, and wanted to lead with her when the war was over, whenever that may be. It was last Christmas, now it was next Christmas. Some soldiers had a look on their face that said it would never be over. This was the new world, and this was how it was going to be, from now on.

'Attenshun'! Platoon, fall out!' Jim's reminiscing was broken into as the column of men came to a halt. He had not noticed the change in scenery around him, but looked around now. They were on the edge of a large village, tents had been set up in the fields outside, and what looked like a clearing station in a field separate. He knew looking around that the few houses would be commandeered, if that had not been so already, by the soldiers higher up the ladder than him. As the men milled around, some sat down to rest, some stood chatting, and others slowly moved off towards the large tents, the same as they had seen when they were training back in England.

'Like being back in England… if it were not for the boche shooting at us!'

Archie slapped Jim on the back, and he moved towards the fields. The two had become quite close since arriving in France, living in similar villages back in England, and Archie working the land. The same level headedness was attributed to both lads by their colleagues and superiors, but Archie was more outgoing and positive than Jim, making them a good team. Jim followed, as a tight column of men from moments before now spread towards the camping field, keen to relax and then see what, if anything, the village had to offer for the few days and hours they were due to be here.

The sun had set when the two comrades in arms walked out of the mess tent and towards the village. Evening had fallen, and after the rain of the day the night sky was now clear, and full of stars. Jim looked up, and wondered about his family and Bea, and what they would be doing now, under these very same stars.

'You can't help them now, Jim, just keep yourself alive'. He turned and saw Archie looking at him, smoking a woodbine. 'Let's just keep our heads and get out of this bloody war. And to do that, we need a drink!' He punched Jim on the shoulder, and their pace quickened as they hurried into the village square, wanting to make the most of their time away from the front line.

There was a large café still open, in the centre of the village round a small square with the remains of a fountain in the centre. Unsurprisingly it was busy, but not packed full of soldiers, the rest of the regiment obviously finding other locations to spend the little money they had in finding a way to forget the war for a few hours, alcohol or women. He also noticed a small group of ambulance drivers at a table by the door, men and women, engrossed in some story one of them was relaying. Jim commandeered a dust covered table for two in the corner, slightly away from the main rumble of noise in the further corner of the café, where a corporal was trying to get a tune out of an old piano that looked like it had seen as much action in the war as any soldier on either side.

As usual the first glass went down in a few seconds, and the second was poured before they started to talk, the edge of the last few days taken off by the alcohol. Conversation flowed, as they talked about home, and gossip they had heard, anything but the actual conflict itself. That they had tried to leave behind with every footstep on the march. The second glass was drunk, and another bottle ordered from the waiter.

'I think I will go after this. I just need sleep, if I can get it'. Jim's face betrayed his condition, and the tired, worn look was mirrored in his friends.

'Jesus, we only just got here. C'mon mate, just stay out an hour. Looks like the fella knows a tune, even if it sounds dreadful on that thing!'

'Maybe', Jim replied, caught between wanting to stay out and enjoy a bit of freedom for the first time in weeks, maybe months, and wanting to just let sleep wash over him, taking with it the knowledge of where he was and what he had been doing… and what he would go back to do.

He lifted his glass of wine to his mouth to take a swig, and tiredly lifted his eyes as the bell on the door to the café jingled and another couple of female ambulance drivers entered. The glass hovered by his lips, as he watched them look briefly around, then move towards the table of their friends in the service Jim had spotted earlier.

One of the girls was short and stocky, long blonde hair and an infectious laugh that appeared as soon as they reached the table. But it was the other he stared at. Quite tall and slim, long black hair that was tied up in a bun. He had only seen her on profile walking from the door, but for all that he knew who it was immediately. The glass was returned to the table, and Jim stood, mumbling something to Archie before heading across the room.

'Oooh, got an admirer I think' said one of the male drivers to the woman Jim moved to stand behind, and Bea turned to look up.

'Jim!' She was on her feet in an instant, but then they both became coy, not sure what to do or say after months apart, and in a place they had never been together before. 'Let's go outside, I will be back in a minute', this last directed at the table, as she led Jim to the door outside.

'I will be back later' he managed to shout to an open mouthed Archie as they both exited the café. Outside, alone, it was easier, away from the clamour and noise of the café.

'What are you doing here, Bea? How on.. why? Why are you…what made…'

'Why don't you try one question at a time, Jim?' she smiled, 'let's go over to the fountain, we are in the way here'. They moved across and sat on the edge, Jim not taking his eyes off her face. 'I should have said, but I did not want you to worry. I'm sorry. The next job fell through, they moved to the country for the duration, and were going to take on a tutor locally. So I was out of a job, and had to make a choice'. She kissed him on the cheek, and then they kissed properly.

'Sorry, I would not wait much longer! Anyway, I could have gone home, but there is no work there, just back to maybe being a maid. Or then I saw they were advertising for ambulance drivers. With most of the men signing up, they couldn't be choosy, I guess. There are a few conscientious objectors in our group, but it is mainly us girls.'

'How long have you been her? I had no idea? Why did you not write?'

'I did not want to worry you, and I did not know if it would happen. But I wanted to do my bit, and really there was not a great choice! This or nothing.'

Archie appeared at the door, along with the blonde girl that Jim had seen Bea enter with. 'I think we are wanted! I will just tell Archie to wait'.

'No, I have to go, we are on duty in half an hour, we just came out for some air. When do you go back?'

'The day after tomorrow'

'I am on duty all night, but then have a day and evening off. Let me sleep tomorrow and I can meet you late afternoon? Here, about four?'

'Yes, no problem at all. Bea, take care, you will be alright?' The short time together had let the concern that Jim had buried rise to the surface again.

'I have been here a month, I know what I am doing, please don't worry!' She gave him another kiss on the cheek.

'I still can't believe it's you? My god Bea, I wondered what was going on, if I would see you again.'

'And here I am! You can't get rid of me!' The flippancy in her voice betrayed by the tear in the corner of her eye, they held hands and crossed back over the road, dodging the mingling soldiers and locals moving around the square. 'See you tomorrow', and Bea was gone with her friend, leaving Jim with Archie, whose face told him he wanted to know everything, and now!

The next day passed by slowly. Jim had gotten Archie up to date the evening before.

'Jesus, I am not sure I would want my girl out here? I mean, it's a war Jim, it's not like a day out at the beach?'

Although he hid it behind some bravado, Jim could not agree more. He knew Bea was more worldly wise than him, and she was far more intelligent than him, and unlikely to make a silly mistake. But they were only mere miles from the battlefield. Last night, you could hear the guns as it if were at the end of the field. And she was on duty driving towards that.

The morning was spent cleaning his kit, and the afternoon playing football and watching the time tick by on his watch. He left Archie towards the middle of the afternoon and walked towards the village centre, with a 'Behave yourself!' being flung at his back as he walked off, that made him smile. After speaking to the Lieutenant on the way, he was still a few minutes early. Looking up, he saw her walking towards him, her friend from the night before in tow, but they parted when they saw he was alone, and Bea greeted him with a hug.

'Shall we walk? I only woke an hour ago, I need to stretch my legs.'

Heading towards the south of the village, they cut down a side street and headed towards the river, away from the hustle of the buildings and found some peace and quiet.

'How was your shift?' Even now, the war still kick started the conversation. 'I heard the bombardment'.

'It was a short lived one, I think they just wanted our boys to know they were still there. About three runs, reserve line back here to the clearing station. A quiet one, if I am honest.'

Jim looked at her, and thought as much as she may underplay it, you could see the last few months she had endured in her eyes. No sparkle, or brightness he had always seen, or thought he could see. She looked older already, or was that just the time apart? He looked away, aware he had been staring, and looked down the river.

'How are you? I am sorry, we have barely spoken, last night was such a rush!'.. He smiled, kissed her on the lips, and brought her up to date on what had happened since he joined up, adding detail to the letters he had already sent. In turn, Bea spoke about the village, his parents, and her journey to the front.

'I still can't believe you did not tell me? But I should have guessed… you were never going to go home after London?'

'No, I am sorry, but once you were not coming, and I lost the new job, I had to change plan. I wanted to help, wanted to do my bit, and here I can. You're not angry?'

'Of course not…I was never going to be able to tell you what to do anyway! You always knew what you wanted. I worry about your safety, I guess that's the problem… until now I knew you and my grandparents and my mother were home safe in England. It was like I was alone, an orphan maybe, with only myself to worry about. Now you are here, I don't know how I feel. So happy to see you, stupidly happy, but worried too.' Jim looked away at the river, trying to hide his feelings, mixed up as they were since the moment he saw her the night before.

'Let's go and get a bite to eat', Bea stood up, brushed her uniform off and started to move away. 'It's getting colder and I need to eat!'

They went to the Café they had been at just a day before. Bea noticed how quickly the first couple of glasses of wine went down with Jim, before he slowed and started to relax.

'Do you think of the future?'

The question was raised by Jim as he finished the last morsel of food on his plate, trying to come to terms with having Bea with him, and reconciling that with the fact she was no longer following the plan they had made through no fault of her own.

'I do, but rarely. This is what I do now, I can help, I am wanted, needed even. I feel I am contributing. But yes, I can see me going back, tutoring again'. She pushed her plate away and held his hand across the table. 'I still want our future. I still want London, and I miss teaching children. That's still who I am' she said wistfully. 'But it has to be with you there. Will it be, that's the question'?

'I'm sorry, I struggle with this. So much has happened in the last six months. I have seen so much, stuff I wish I hadn't. I can't look beyond the war, I can't see what it will be like. It seems, I dunno, far away? Like it's not real. But I do know I want it to be with you, whenever or wherever that is. I just don't know when, or how'. He stared into his glass, as if the answer lay at the bottom, if only he could look harder. 'I wish I did'.

The door crashed open as a group of soldiers entered, and the peace of the café was shattered by men wanting to enjoy as much as possible their few hours left of freedom. Jim acknowledged a couple he knew, then signaled to Bea it was probably a good time to go, leaving some money on the table they both moved towards the door and out onto the street. The cold air and near pitch black surprised them as emerged out onto the street.

'When do you need to go back?'

'I am free tonight, not on duty until the morning, the girls know I am with you'

Jim was glad to hear this, taking Bea's hand in his and heading down the road. 'If you want, you can stay with me, only if you want to, mind. Our lieutenant has a room, and kindly, for an un-godly supply of woodbines, has said I can have it for the night. I have to be back 7am'.

He stopped talking, aware he was starting to gabble, and looked at Bea in the dark, trying to determine her response from the vague form of her face a few inches away. 'I think I can agree to that' she answered, squeezing his hand as they moved along the road.

The building was towards the edge of the village, and after struggling to find it in the dark for a few minutes, they were soon inside the building and up the stairs. The room was spartan, an old, large bed that had seen better days, no shutters, but the remains of curtains that Jim pulled to give them some sort of privacy. He could see why the Lieutenant had pushed for this room when he was billeted, and had tried to keep it tidy in the short time he was in it. Edge of town, the opposite side to the Front, it looked away from the war, and was as quiet as anywhere could be in this part of France.

Bea entered behind him, and latched the door.

Chapter 21

Darkness. Peace. Then Jim's eyes opened as if they had been surprised into it. Mud filled his vision. The quiet of the battlefield a stark contrast to the harrowing noise of earlier. He closed his eyes again, took a deep breath, then slowly opened them again, turning his head so his cheek rested on the earth. Archie was about six feet away. Immediately the image of him turning to face Jim in the carnage appeared in his mind's eye, and he was glad his friend's back was to him. Jim could see that he himself was just below the rim of the crater he had fallen into, maybe a couple of feet below the surface.

The next thing he felt was the ache in his leg, announcing itself as his body slowly woke up to the situation. Looking down, he saw a gash in his right thigh, where the blood has started to congeal, about three inches across. He thought it looked superficial… he had stitched up worse cuts on his rounds as a veterinary assistant, and various horses and dogs and soon healed good as new. Of course, they had not been sat in the mud and misery of northern France. Jim reached into his inside pocket, and took out a bandage, tying it quickly round this thigh. It was really not enough, but it would have to do until he could get it seen to.

He looked around, avoiding Archie, but knowing he would have to go there before he tried to make his way back to the lines. The crater was around twenty five feet across, and around ten deep, with a couple of feet of water at the bottom. A couple of bodies lay on the opposite side, victims from the same fight as he was, judging from the uniforms. Jim remembered from the remnants of barbed wire and wood he had seen in front it when he was running, the trenches were maybe fifty feet behind him… in the quiet he told himself he could almost hear the murmur of chatter calling him back. And he had to go back. No one would be sent out to recover bodies until darkness had fallen, and he had no intention of staying here any longer than he had to.

Putting it off no longer, he crawled the few feet through the mud to where Archie's body lay. He paused, not wanting to carry on, but then he pulled him over from his side onto his back, only allowing himself to see the shattered face through the very edges of his vision. Un-buttoning his friends tunic, he reached in and took out the letters and photos they both knew each kept in the same place, and took the ring from his wedding finger. Finally he took the identification tags from around his neck, before running his fingers down his friend's eyes to close them, then covering his face with his tin hat. He wanted to do more. It did not seem enough. He closed his eyes and offered up a brief prayer, knowing if he was going to move it had to be soon. 'I'm sorry'.

'Help me!'

Barely more than a whisper, Jim thought he had imagined it. Confusedly he looked down at his friends tin helmet covered face, but knew as he did so the voice had obviously not come from there. The sound of rain drops hitting puddles started, the sky darkening again, as if trying to paint a veil over the horror that had again been wrought across the countryside. Jim lifted his head ever so slightly, cocking his ear, as the sound came again.

'Please!'

Turning round, he looked at the two bodies he has seen moments before on the opposite side of the rim, and saw the one on the left had tried to lift itself up onto its arm, head lifting ever so slightly towards him. Jim's eyes widened as he realised what looked earlier like a lifeless body was now moving ever so slightly.

Looking round, he had planned to move around the opposite way to where the other Tommy lay, but changed his mind immediately, and with a passing glance at his friend's form, started to slither on his belly and hands and knees towards the other figure, keeping his head as low as he could. It took barely a minute, though the short time seemed to drag interminably, and in that period he heard not a sound, just the odd word coming from the figure lay before him. The private's face was covered in blood, he had the lower part of his right arm missing, and as Jim looked down his left leg there just seemed to be a mass of blood.

'Don't worry mate, I'll get you out, just hold steady', the words coming automatically out of his mouth, that his minds was not yet sure how he would make that happen. He looked back up at his fallen comrade, who turned his face up at the same time, and Jim found himself staring into the eyes of Tom Smith.

'Jim? My god, it's Jim Turner!' The words came out in a rush, and ended in a gasp as whatever unseen damage done to the man lay on the ground made itself known. Tom put his head back down and screwed his eyes shut, waiting for the pain to pass. Both men sat there, not moving, Jim keeping an eye on the ground surrounding the crater, as the bully of his youth struggled to overcome the pain enveloping him. Jim moved a few feet to the right, where the edge of the hole they were in dripped twelve inches or so, and peered through the gap, seeing the allied line was between fifty and sixty feet away, further than he first thought. A couple of smaller craters dotted the route, a man could cover the ground quickly, using them for cover on the way. But two men?

'I thought I had seen you'.

Jim worked his way back to Tom, sliding back through the mud, head working out the options open to him, to them, as he moved.

'Wasn't sure…. Not one hundred percent….you've changed.' Tom gasped for breath between each few words, and Jim wondered what damage had been done that he could not see, though to his eyes the leg at least looked like it would need to be amputated. And the gash on his forehead. Jim tried to stop thinking about it.

'Don't bother....no.....point....' Jim looked down to see Tom staring up at him. 'I won't ..... get ..... halfway ..... pain's .... too much'.

The rain became heavier, and for a few moments the two men stood looking at each other, Tom's head now back on the ground, the strength to do that no longer in his body.

'I'm sorry...' He stared into Jim's eyes. 'It's not....worth.... anything now, but.... I am sorry'.

The words seemed to cut into Jim. He had been hoping, he realized in that moment, that he could just wait a few minutes for Tom to die, and then he could just go back on his own. But he was not going to do that. He was better than that. Even if his charge died on the way, he would get him back to the lines.

'You're coming with me, Tom, then you can apologise properly back in England'. Jim reached into Tom's tunic, noticing as he did that it looked like he was unconscious. Taking out the bandage, he cut it in two with his knife, tying one half round the head, and the other round his lower arm. It would never be enough, but it would have to do, surmising the leg would not be worth the effort, as it looked like nothing would save that now.

On his back, the rain so heavy now it was like a mist, meaning that Jim was unable to see more than ten or twelve yards, he grabbed Tom and pulled him towards the opening on the crater ridge he had looked through before.

'You're coming back Tom, get used to it!'. He received a soft grunt in reply, and figured that was good enough for now.

He turned and looked through the gap back to the lines, not visible now, but he knew where they were. There was a sap, he knew, to the left, but he would have to walk just as far to reach that.

Best to take the direct route. Tom moaned again. He would have to chance it, and head at first for the smaller crater nearer to the lines.

'C'mon Tom, time to go'.

Jim didn't want to delay, so scooped him up in his arms and immediately started a stumbling run towards the lines. The expected rattle of gunfire or rifle shots did not occur, and yard by yard the distance left to go reduced. His legs shuffled one in front of the other, trying to stoop to keep himself a smaller target, but also having to under the dead weight of the man he carried. Twice falling to his knees, the pain from his wound exploding each time, he managed to get up and stumble on, waiting for the end to come.

A rifle shot cracked and Jim was sure he felt the disturbance in the air as the bullet whistled past his face, belatedly realizing it had come from his own lines. 'Shit!' He stumbled the last few yards before throwing Tom and himself forward into cover, slithering through the mud and pooled water of a shallower pit, as another shot immediately sounded above his head.

Jim turned and rolled Tom over. In the streaming rain and darkened sky he could not tell if he had changed colour, or was lucid at all, but putting his cheek to his mouth he could feel some shallow breaths coming out.

'Good lad, not far to go.'

He turned and crawled a couple of yards to the front of the shallow pit they had stumbled into, and called towards the line, just loud enough for them to hear.

'It's Jim Turner. I'm coming in with Tom Smith. Don't fire!'

'Jim! Jesus Christ, I thought I had shot you!'. Jim heard shouts to hold fire being passed along each part of the line, then the same voice shouted 'Come on, do it now!'

Jim turned back to Tom, lifted him for a finale time and stumbled forward across the mud. Looking at the lines for the first time since first lifting him, he was startled at how close they were, and after a few seconds he slid to a stop, and dropped to his knees. Hands appeared from below and took Tom, letting Jim turn and fall down into the trench.

The stress and exhaustion of the last fifteen minutes, on top of the earlier battle and the death of Archie now engulfed him, as Jim's knees buckled and tears started to flow down his face. For a moment he could not stop, it was if everything that had happened since he joined up had been bottled up and this morning's events had just released the stopper. He sat and sobbed, until he felt an arm on his shoulder, and a lit woodbine appeared in front of his face.

'You'll be all right, son. Take your time'. Jim took a drag, wiped his eyes as well as he could and scrambled to his feet. He looked at the Lieutenant in front of him, the same one whose room he had borrowed the last time he saw Bea.

'How's Tom?'

The figure in front of him did not speak, just stood to one side and Jim saw the a figure lay on a stretcher, the bearers quickly tightening bandages before lifting the dead weight and running off away down the trench.

'Breathing. But how long for I could not say.' He walked away, pausing a few yards away. 'Get yourself cleaned up and that cut seen to. Well done'.

Jim's eyes followed him as he disappeared along down the trench.

Chapter 22

Jim moved down the support lines to the reserve trench, getting his leg treated when there, nothing more than stitches in the gash, and bandages. Every man was needed and he was put on light duties, but back in the front line. The latest gossip was that there were no more advances planned, then the next round would be saying that they were due to go over the top the next day. Jim listened without taking it in. He wrote to Archie's family, as they both said they would for each other, sending with the letter the personal effects he had taken. Within a few days the events of the last advance over the top had been buried. He was sure they would be back at some point in the future. He just did not want to think about them now, it was all too raw. Best to concentrate on the next few moments, minutes, hours.

Front line life carried on as before, days of mundanity, interspersed with periods of terror during bombardments. The next advance was sure to come at some point, and Jim found he was living in the hope that he would get his leave before it happened, or at least some time in reserve, so that he could see Bea. He knew she was still working in the same area, ferrying wounded back from the front line. They still wrote daily, sometimes twice. He would sit slumped on the fire step, cup of warm water masquerading as tea alongside him, and read her letters over and over again, before taking his time to reply. Some passages were just emptying his heart onto the page, some worried and worked over time and again to make them just right.

'Turner!'

Jim looked up from reading Bea's latest letter, only received that morning but already the paper appeared months older than it was, writing smudged from folding and unfolding, creases down the centre and thumbprints on the corners. Jim looked up and saw the Captain, and immediately stood to attention and saluted.

'Don't worry, at ease. Just got some good news for you, thought you might like to know straight away. Five days leave. Should be long enough to get back to England and see your folks'. He handed Jim the orders, and turned to go while Jim read the order. 'Oh, and I have mentioned you in dispatches. Very brave what you did, good man. Carry on'.

Jim watched his Captain walk away, then looked again at the order. It was from the next day, giving him five days out of the front line. He wanted to go home, but wanted to see Bea too. Maybe she was due some time off for herself? They could go back together, kill two birds with one stone? The ideas quickly flew round his head. He sat down, took out pen and paper, and quickly wrote a note to Bea. Short and succinct, he told her about the leave, and the time he would be back in the village they had last met in. If she could get time off, he could get his papers back to England there, and if she could not, he would stay with her.

Jim quickly sealed the note and gave it to the runner, along with a message, and passed him the charge, a couple of squares of chocolate and a woodbine. He knew the runner would be taking messages back tonight, and would pass this on to the Red Cross Hospital that Bea was working in. With any luck she would get it before mid-day tomorrow.

His task done, Jim walked back down the trench. The afternoon and evening lay before him, snippets of conversation had with people around him, but his mind was on the letter and seeing Bea the next day. Eventually, after his period on as lookout, Jim slept fitfully through of the night.

Bea made her final journey at the end of her shift back to the main hospital and clearing station in the village. It had been a quiet night, just one journey taking six badly wounded soldiers to the train station in the next town. The journey was slow, and Bea aware that every pothole and bump in the road only caused more pain to the men in her charge, so as always she was torn between the need to get them there quickly, but the quicker the journey the harder it was for them. Even after weeks of this she still cringed deep inside at every moan, groan and muffled scream that came from the back of the vehicle. She doubted she would every really get used to it.

The soldiers were taken off and loaded onto the train by the porter helping her, a male conscientious objector who did all the heavy lifting, though for Bea his best trait by far was his reticence to talk. She liked to be left alone to think on these journeys, it was the time when she got some peace and to think, if peace was the right word to use.

Bea got back to base just before ten, nigh on at the end of her shift. She said goodnight to her colleague, and thanked him for his help, receiving a grunt and a nod in return. Which is more than normal, she thought to herself. She sighed, and moved toward the larger tent to the side, that was used as a sort of office for the staff.

'Good journey?' The matron was sat at a desk with a pile of paperwork to one side. Bea liked her, though to the others working there she could be officious and had a tendency to be abrupt. That was what was needed in this situation though, she thought, and the two had always rubbed along nicely. In turn the Matron saw the hard worker in Bea, and somebody who wanted to make the most of themselves and the chances life gave them. The respect therefore was mutual, and she gave Bea more support that some of the others, who she could pick out immediately… those who thought it was some sort of game, or who came purely so that they could say they had done it, then as soon as they could would try to get back to their other lives.

'Yes, it seems quiet. I am not sure all six will make it back, but they are on their way'.

Bea was thinking of one soldier in particular, who seemed to be defying his injuries in staying alive, though she was not sure what sort of life that would be in the future.

'It's those that keep fighting and stay awake that survive'. The matron nodded towards the post trays that lined one side of the canvas room. 'You've got a letter, saw the boy drop it in earlier, and thought I would mention it before you got to bed'.

'Thank you'.

Bea picked it up and walked out of the room and back to her quarters. Sitting on her bed, she ripped open the envelope, recognizing the writing, and knowing anyway that Jim would be the only one writing to her, especially hand delivered as this obviously was. As soon as she finished reading it, she was back out of the tent and heading towards the Matron.

'Yes, you can take leave. You are overdue it, and everyone is back on duty from six in the morning'. She glanced at Bea knowingly, and took a sip of tea from the mug in front of her. 'I may be old but I am not stupid. A hand delivered letter, seeing you check your post morning and night. You're papers will be done by the morning, five days. Make sure you come back, you're the most reliable person out of all of them'.

'Thank you!'

Bea would have said more, but the older lady was engrossed in further paperwork and oblivious to her again. It was only later she would realise in the thrill of receiving the leave she had completely missed the compliment paid her, listening to her other colleagues this was arguably the first and last time the matron had given anyone a positive word.

Bea rushed back to her quarters she shared with the other female drivers, and packed the few things she would need to take back to England. As Jim had said in his brief letter, that was the best option, they could be together and see the family, as hard as that would be for him.

Chapter 23

The day dawned bright and clear. Jim had slept fitfully, but it did not matter. As soon as it was light he busied himself with washing, shaving and cleaning his teeth as best he could, a practice he had tried to keep up for all difficulty of maintaining it. It was the first thing his mother would comment on, he knew!

Packing his kit quickly and quietly, he said 'cheerio' to the men in his company staying. There was a group of them on leave who he had fought alongside in this part of the line, and they left at six on the dot, moving down the communication trench towards the reserve lines. There was a transport leaving that would take them back to the village he had last spent a few days in with Bea, and then from there a further transport back to the next town and the train to the coast. At least I am saved the march, mused Jim, as the line of men exited the trench and walked toward the open truck that waited them, leaving the hustle of front line life behind them. He could almost feel he shoulders start to relax, as he looked forward to a few days away from the front.

Pack on the seat under him, Jim looked back at the lines where he had spent so much of the last few months. The desire to get moving was great, and he looked around at the other men, chatting animatedly as they waited for the off, jokes and laughter filling the air. The soldier by him smiled and offered him a woodbine.

Taking the cigarette, he looked around him, becoming aware of a roar that seemed to surround him, briefly accompanied by a piercing, whistle like sound. He looked at the soldier sat opposite, briefly took in the widening eyes. 'Get ou….!', then darkness enveloped him.

He came to, briefly. Flat on his back, head turned to one side. He seemed stuck, unable to move. The feeling he should not try to flashed up in his mind. He could feel heat from somewhere. Dark smoke billowed around them. Shouting. Feet running out of view….then the smoke dispersed slightly and a body came into view a few feet in front of his face, then another. The taste of blood in his mouth. Like that time Tom punched him… Tom, who was possibly dead now. His rifle, where was his rifle, he would be in trouble if he lost it. He turned his head to look but found he could not….his eyes closed and the darkness enshrined him again.

The feeling of being lifted. Someone groaned…. he realized it was him. Jim's eyes opened a fraction, and he could see the men either side of the stretcher he was on. Wisps of smoke still wafted around. He did not think he could feel anything below his waist. His back felt wet. He knew where he was going… he would see Bea, but not how he planned. He could feel the wetness spread, his blood he assumed. The stretcher stopped. 'Jesus Christ, we've got to stop this!'…. Jim closed his eyes, thinking he should save his energy, and open them when he saw Bea again.

Chapter 24

The train slowed, the station a few hundred metres distant. It was busy, all the carriages packed with visitors. The usual scramble as people got to their feet, grabbing luggage from the overhead racks. A mixture of people, from all walks of life, judging from their attire. She waited, there was no rush. Looking up, she saw an older man in the seat opposite, they had briefly spoken at the last station. They caught each other's expression, and he smiled and rolled his eyes, and she returned the smile, both of them amused by the shared knowledge that nothing would change, regardless of how quickly you got off the train.

Bea stood eventually, helped her companion and then grabbed their one bag from above her head. The other man, whose name she could not quite remember, let her out with a smile, and the three of them moved off the train, the last to get off. As expected there was still a queue to get off the station.

'Are you both staying long?'

'No, we will go back tonight, we have a hotel room booked in Calais, and will get the early morning crossing. I don't want to be away from home too long'. The man nodded.

'It's the best way. You can't change what happened, and you have to carry on and look after yourself.' He looked at her companion. 'And your family. Well, I will leave you here. If I don't see you on the way back, have a safe journey'. He shook her hand, and moved forward through the crowd flowing out of the station.

Bea hung back, not wanting to rush, and not wanting to push and jostle. It did not seem the right thing to do, though that did not seem to bother others. The wait was justified, the walk to their destination she knew was only a mile or so, and the group of people had spread out as most arrivals walked up a slight incline, away from the station and the edge of the town it was situated on.

Bea held her companions hand, as they walked up road in the early spring sunshine. It had been years since she had been here. She let her mind wander back to the day she had waited for Jim at the hospital on the front line. And then the ambulance driving toward her. She knew before it had even stopped that he was on it, and she stood, staring, as the porters rushed around taking the men… the bodies…. off the vehicle. Bea refused to remember any more than that.

She had left France early in the war. When she reached home, she had a constant urge to return, but after the hostilities had finished, she found she could not bring herself to do it. There was always a reason, or an excuse. She was not sure how it would affect her… Bea had tried to move on, she had to…. but would a return help or hinder? She could never be sure.

Eventually she had just put the decision to one side, and carried on with life. Moving back to the village with her parents, got a job at the Manor House cleaning, and helped out at the school. It was as though the five years since she had left there had never happened. Had her life moved forward or not? What had happened to the young girl who wanted as much as she could from her life, and to do everything she wanted to? But she was content, or as content as she would ever be. But the decision was still there to be made, an itch that would not go away, and the one thing that still seemed to keep her awake at night.

Jim's Granddad had made the decision, or suggested the answer in such a way as there really seemed to be no choice. All of his family were still close, and treated her as one of their own.

'You will always miss him, love. He will always be in here with us all', he stated, putting his hand on his own chest. 'You can make a choice on your behalf, arguing the case either way. But can you make a decision on your daughter's behalf?'

Bea looked down at her daughter, holding her hand. Six years old now, and she saw Jim reflected in her every day, though others said how they saw Bea more than anything. And that is how it should be. She was old enough now to be asking more and more questions about Daddy, and if she was honest, Bea was feeling the pull of France more every day. The timing was right.

'Come on, let's go in, we are here'.

They reached the cemetery, and followed a straggling row of people in, slowly, silently walking up and down the rows, each consumed by their own remorse, sorrow, guilt even. Bea followed holding her daughters hand. Hundreds of white crosses, some with names, some not. And she knew there were larger memorials across northern France, with numbers growing as bodies continued to be unearthed daily.

Bea was starting to lose faith, as they walked up and down, until in the middle of the row, almost exactly in the centre of the cemetery, they found what they came to see. A plain, simple white cross, with 'Pvt. J Turner', his rank and date he died.

'Here it is, this is Daddy's grave'. Bea knelt down, her daughter mimicking her, sweeping her dark hair out of her face, her blue eyes wandering from the cross to her Mums face. Bea opened her bag, and took out a single white rose, brought as she got onto the train earlier, and placed it on the grave.

'Why did you buy a rose, mummy?' .

'Because that's something your father gave to me at a very special time in our lives. And it's why I called you Rose'. Rose smiled, and looked back at the grave.

'Goodbye Daddy'. She stood up and put her hand on her Mum's shoulder.

Bea smiled at her, a tear on her cheek, then looked back at the stark wooden cross. Just a name and a number. Nothing that would ever describe or reflect enough about the man who it represented.

'Goodbye Jim Turner. I love you'.

Bea stood, held Rose's hand, and they slowly made their way back down through the rows of white crosses, towards the road, and the station beyond.